How would Riley's lips feel against hers?

Catherine's pulse quickened when she thought about the end of their evening. Would he kiss her good-night? That was the American tradition, wasn't it?

Royal protocol in her country called for first dates to be chaperoned, and a chaste handshake was all any suitor was allowed. Catherine had thanked the heavens for the strict etiquette many times over the years.

But tonight? Tonight she was grateful that no chaperone was watching her every move. Tonight she was hoping—*praying*—for a kiss.

Would it be soft? Warm? Moist? Firm? Slow and languorous? Or furiously ardent? If she had a say, she'd prefer to experience his kiss in each of those forms. The thought had her grinning.

"What are you thinking?" he asked.

"Oh, nothing. Nothing at all."

Nothing she could tell him, anyway…

DONNA CLAYTON

is the recipient of the Diamond Author Award
For Literary Achievement as well as two Holt
Medallions. She's a bestselling author, having made
both the Waldenbooks and B. Dalton series bestseller
lists. She became a writer through her love of reading.
As a child, she marveled at the ability to travel the
world, experience swashbuckling adventures and meet
amazingly bold and daring people without ever leaving
the shade of the huge oak in her very own backyard.
This love of reading sparked in her a passion for
creating "flesh and blood" characters, and storylines
that enable heroes and heroines to learn and grow and
open their hearts to love. In her opinion, love *is* what
makes the world go 'round. She takes great pride in
knowing that, through her work, she provides her
readers the chance to indulge in some purely selfish
romantic entertainment.

One of her favorite pastimes is traveling. Her
other interests include walking, reading, visiting
with friends, teaching Sunday school, cooking and
baking, and she still collects cookbooks, too. In fact,
her house is overrun with them. Donna lives in
Delaware with her husband of twenty-six years.

Donna had a grand time writing this LOGAN'S
LEGACY royal romp, and she hopes her fans have
just as much fun reading this lighthearted adventure.
Please write to Donna care of Silhouette Books. She'd
love to hear from you!

LOGAN'S LEGACY

ROYAL SEDUCTION
DONNA CLAYTON

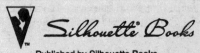
Silhouette Books

Published by Silhouette Books
America's Publisher of Contemporary Romance

Special thanks and acknowledgment are given
to Donna Clayton for her contribution
to the LOGAN'S LEGACY series.

SILHOUETTE BOOKS

ISBN 0-373-61399-7

ROYAL SEDUCTION

2004

Be a part of

Logan's Legacy

*Because birthright has its privileges
and family ties run deep.*

A doctor and a princess share a passion
that defies expectation. And when duty
and desire clash, they have to make the
ultimate decision for their future! Will
love conquer the crown?

Dr. Riley Jacobs: When he met Catherine for
a consultation, he was dazzled by her beauty
but resentful that a healthy person would take
the precious time of a serious doctor. But as he got
to know her, he saw the tender heart of a woman
who crept into his soul....

Princess Catherine von Husden: This free-
spirited princess ran from her royal responsibilities
and delved into Portland's social world. With
her passionate reaction to Portland General's
Dr. Riley Jacobs, Catherine was thinking of
ditching the crown altogether!

No Love Lost? During Dr. Richie's tenure at
the Healthy Living Clinic, couples came together
thanks to his special oil. With his departure, would
love survive? Turn the pages and find out!

THE SOLUTION YOU'VE BEEN WAITING FOR...

THE REMEDY YOU DESERVE...

NoWAIT

THE AMAZING NEW DIET OIL. USE IT AND WATCH THE POUNDS MELT AWAY!

NoWait: A little rub on the skin, and in no time you're thin!

SPONSORED BY THE HEALTHY LIVING CLINIC
IN AFFILIATION WITH PORTLAND GENERAL HOSPITAL
PORTLAND, OREGON

Use as directed
Some side effects may occur
Check with your physician before applying

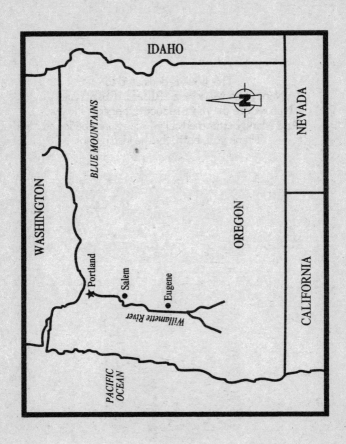

This book is dedicated to
Nancy and Mark ~~Ruz...Ruszes~~...Ruszczycky.
Nan, you're the most seductive princess I know.
And Mark, better medical advice cannot be found.
Thank you, both, for the inspiration!

Prologue

"I'm not marrying that man!" If Princess Catherine von Husden were still a child, she'd have stomped her foot and jutted her chin toward her father. But now that she was twenty-six, such antics were no longer an option. Her only recourse was to fix her eyes on him and refuse to back down.

"Oh, Daddy," her sister droned with irritating complaint, "can't you do something about her?" Yvonne leveled a glare in Catherine's direction. "Cat, you're the oldest. Protocol calls for you to marry first. You know Hampstead and I have been waiting for nearly a year! Just marry Étienne and get it over with."

Catherine calmly remarked, "You shouldn't have waited. And you shouldn't wait any longer. Haven't I always said etiquette be damned?"

Yvonne gasped. Their father's jaw tensed.

Catherine narrowed her eyes on her father. "Besides, the only reason you want a wedding is to try to show up Max. But that's not going to happen. No matter how hard we try, Lextanyans cannot outshine a wedding and a coronation."

Catherine was so happy for her cousin Max. Last year he'd married the love of his life and then had been crowned king of Lantanya. The wedding, attended by the entire von Husden family, had been a glorious affair. And as custom dictated, the coronation had been elaborate in the extreme.

"I wish you'd give up this silly competition." Catherine lifted one hand, palm up. "Uncle Maxwell, may he rest in peace, isn't even around any longer to compete with you." Although Maxwell the Fourth, the former king of neighboring Lantanya, wasn't her father's brother, the two men had been close enough that the man had always been affectionately referred to as "uncle" by Catherine and her sister. Everyone knew about the silly game of one-upmanship that her father and Uncle Maxwell had spent years playing. "And Max doesn't care to compete with you—"

"Catherine, this has nothing to do with me and my cousin, and it certainly has nothing to do with Max," her father said. "This only has to do with you and Étienne. He is an exceptional young man. He's industrious, and he has an excellent background as well as a flawless reputation."

This had her brows arching. "So you haven't heard the stories that he's a skirt-chasing misogynist? Is that what you want me dealing with for the rest of my days?"

Her sister clicked her tongue in dismay. "Cat, that's your future husband you're talking about."

"Oh, no." Despite her intention to remain unruffled, determination—along with an unexpected stirring of alarm—had her pulling her arms tight across her chest. "The man may be handsome as the devil himself, and he may be highly educated. He may even have a noble or two climbing around in his family tree." Cat halted abruptly, gasping with a sudden revelation. "He's offering you the Caslow Diamond, isn't he?" The diamond was huge, and world-renowned. One look at her father's face was proof enough. She shook her head. "I can't believe I'm being traded for a glittery rock." Her spine stiffened with renewed resolve. "I don't care what he's offering. I will not spend my time keeping tabs on a hound dog of a husband who's sniffing around other women at every opportunity. That's not what marriage is supposed to be about."

"You know nothing about marriage." Her father's tone went taut. "Étienne's actions before he became interested in a union with you will not be held against him. The man had to live, didn't he?"

Catherine held her ground. However she got the impression that her ground was becoming a tad shaky. Usually, her father's staunch decision would begin to soften under her unfaltering protests. Usually.

But today Prince Wilhelm Adolf was proving why he'd remained regent of Lextanya for so long as his shoulders squared with a frightening fortitude.

"You also know nothing about family loyalty," he continued. "If you did, you wouldn't continue to embarrass the von Husden name by refusing to do as you're told."

His blue eyes were as cold as ice chips, and they sent a chill through Catherine.

"No matter what fantasy has enraptured you this week, Catherine, it's time you wake up. We are of the regal lineage of Lantanya. And we rule Lextanya. The von Husdens are one of the last remaining truly royal houses in the world. We are renowned and respected. And I won't allow you to threaten our reputation ever again, Catherine."

Oh, Lord, would he never allow her to live down that one small slipup? It had been ages ago. She'd been sixteen when it happened, and she hadn't caused him a moment of trouble since. Well, no real trouble, anyway.

"Unlike some nobles," her father added, "our side of the von Husden family has never been tainted with nasty misdeeds."

Certainly he wasn't comparing her childhood prank to Uncle Maxwell's stepbrother's villainous crime against the entire nation of Lantanya? Max's first act as ruler had been to send his step-uncle to prison for high treason.

"People are beginning to talk," her father continued. "About you. Rumor and innuendo can be just as fatal to our royal name as scandalous criminal offenses. Besides, it's completely natural that Lextanyans are beginning to wonder about you, Catherine. You're not getting any younger."

She couldn't believe he was tossing her into the same rotten barrel with a true criminal. And all because she didn't want to marry Étienne. Then again, she guessed she shouldn't be surprised. Her father had always had a poor opinion of her.

"But I don't need a man to make me happy," Catherine said. "I don't need to marry. Go ahead and announce Yvonne's engagement."

Prince Wilhelm ignored her. "We live and die by tradition. The day we release hold on custom is the day our house will fall."

Catherine plopped her fist on her hip. "What a load of imperialistic bunk!"

Yvonne's sob made Catherine spin on her heel.

"Oh, honey, I'm sorry." She went to her sister's side. "I didn't mean any disrespect to Father. Or to our family."

Catherine had been speaking plainly to her father for years; however, she never made a habit of doing so in front of Yvonne, or anyone else for that matter. No, the barbed relationship she and Wilhelm shared was kept private. Just between the two of them. But he was going too far in his attempts to marry her off.

Shrugging Catherine's comforting arm from her shoulder, Yvonne cried, "You're disrespectful of all of us, Cat. Why can't you see that? And you're keeping me from becoming Hampstead's wife!"

"I'm supposed to marry a man I don't love so you can do what you see as your royal duty?" Although Catherine worked hard to restrain the sharpness in her voice, she knew she'd failed.

Her sister clenched her hands into tight, white fists. "You are so selfish." With tears streaming openly down her pale cheeks, Yvonne raced from the room.

Catherine watched her sister disappear through the doorway of her father's office, her chest growing heavy with dread and guilt. The walls were covered, floor to ceiling, with oak panels that had darkened over time, and right now they seemed to close in on her as she turned to face her father.

"Your actions are affecting everyone around you, Catherine." Anger emanated from him in simmering waves. "You are duty bound to do as I bid."

Trepidation overrode all emotion in her. She'd never heard him speak like this before. He'd pleaded and cajoled and threatened, but there had always been something— some unspoken expression or tone—that had left her feeling there was a way out. But that unspoken something wasn't present at the moment, and that scared her.

"Étienne is ready to arrive at any time. All I have to do is call him."

"Father, no!"

"He is the one, Catherine," he pressed. "There *will* be a wedding. A grand affair. It will be your day to shine."

"This is the new millennium." She threw her arms wide. "No one arranges marriages anymore. That idea went out with catapults and chastity belts."

"I've spoken to Étienne on your behalf," he continued smoothly. "When he arrives, he'll expect to spend plenty of time with you during his visit. Your engagement will be announced soon after his visit."

Panic flared inside her like white-hot flames. She wanted to rant and rave, but knew it would do no good, so she pressed her lips together to hold in the churning emotion. Her father's mind was made up, that much was all too clear. He'd even gone behind her back and set his plan into motion. Her dismal future would begin with one phone call.

He went silent waiting for her to respond. She would not agree with his plan. She refused to give him that satisfaction.

"May I go now?" she asked.

He gave a single nod. "Just so long as we understand each other. Duty calls, Catherine. Duty calls. And you, my dear, shall answer."

She wanted to leave. She wanted to run. But she couldn't get her feet to move. The whole world felt as if it were collapsing in on her. What was wrong with her? Yvonne couldn't wait to get married. Couldn't wait to produce a gaggle of royal babies. She didn't need love, it seemed. In fact, Yvonne had been quite happy with the man their father had chosen for her.

So why was she so resistant?

Catherine dashed away the hot tear of frustration. She didn't know why she continued to be defiant. She just felt she had to. And no amount of kingly commands was going to change that.

What she'd like to do was just run away. Go somewhere fun and exciting. Crawl out from under the burdensome von Husden name and all the royal responsibilities that went along with it and enjoy a little purely naughty fun.

But that was impossible.

Duty calls, Catherine. Her father's chilly reminder caused a shiver to course across every inch of her skin. *And you, my dear, shall answer.*

Her jaw firmed, and she wanted to mutter, "Duty be damned." But she held her tongue.

"Is there anything else?" Her father asked, looking up from the paperwork he'd been reviewing.

"I need some time," she blurted.

"I thought we had already concluded that your time had run out."

"Please, Father." She stopped. Swallowed. Took a deep breath. Allowing panic to overwhelm her would be a mistake. She had to make a rational argument. She tried again, "Father, I need some time to get used to the idea of…" She refused to voice the phrase *marrying Étienne,* so instead, she said, "the idea that my life will soon be changing. You're asking a lot of me—"

"I'm asking no more of you than I am of your sister."

"I need some time," she repeated. Alarm began to erode her self-control. She had to say something that would make him agree to give her what she needed. "I'm not asking for the world here. Just two weeks." Then an idea came to her out of the blue and she exclaimed, "To buy a trousseau!"

The straight line that had been his mouth softened.

"It wouldn't look very good if I didn't have all the things I needed to begin—"

"Two weeks, you say?"

"Yes," she told him, relief flooding her.

Prince Wilhelm sighed. "You'll take your sister along?"

Risking more disapproval, Cat shook her head slowly. "Yvonne is very upset with me. I doubt she'd be very much help."

He glanced down at the papers on his desk. "Well, you can't very well go alone."

"I'm not a child. I want to go alone. There's no reason why I shouldn't. I'll go as Catherine Houston."

When each of his children had turned twenty-one, Prince Wilhelm gifted them with a credit card and bank account under an assumed name. Traveling incognito was the perfect way to deflect the barrage of reporters whenever they took mini holidays or went shopping on Oxford Street in London. When your family owned the bank that backed the credit card—when your family owned the whole darned country—you could pretty much do whatever you wanted.

Her father sat down in his overstuffed leather chair. "Where will you go?"

Anxiety had her tossing up her hands. "I don't know. I haven't decided."

"But—"

"This will be the last trip I take as a single woman," she said, a terrible sinking feeling twittering her stomach. "Would you please just give me a little space?"

For a long moment, he stared. And finally he murmured, "You may have two weeks. Two."

One

If the monotony of this job didn't kill him, Dr. Riley Jacobs thought, then the paint fumes would. Taking over the running of Portland General Hospital's new Healthy Living Clinic hadn't been where he'd expected to put his extensive ER training into practice; however, the position had turned out to be a necessary rung on the ladder to where he wanted to go—and he had every intention of reaching his ultimate goal.

Riley thought of himself as a late bloomer, being thirty years old and having just completed his residency at Portland General Hospital. However, he'd received rave reviews from the ER chief of staff, and he'd truly expected a job offer. But instead Riley had been asked by the head honcho, himself—the hospital director—if he would become acting director of the Healthy Living Clinic. It seemed that things had gone quite awry here recently. And

Riley had been told if he could set the mess right and keep bad publicity at bay, then a job would be waiting for him over in the hospital's emergency room. He'd promised to do his best.

The perfunctory knock on his office door had him calling out, "It's open."

Faye Lassen secured a small stack of patient files in the crook of one arm. The thirty-two-year-old woman with a Ph.D. in nutrition and psychology wore her hair pinned up in a neat 'do, and wore a crisp white lab jacket over a navy knee-length skirt. One look at her and the word *professional* popped into one's mind.

"Hi, Riley," she said. "Busy?"

"Just reading through all this paperwork so I'll be ready for our meeting. We should get over to the hospital soon, shouldn't we?"

Anxiety clouded her blue eyes. At least, he thought her eyes were blue. He couldn't be sure since they were hidden for most part behind the iconic, huge-rimmed glasses she wore.

"I don't believe I'm going to be able to make it," she told him.

"What's wrong?"

"I was just alerted that one of my nutritionists has called in sick and I've got a client waiting. If I'd been told ahead of time, I'd have called her and rescheduled her appointment."

Riley set down the papers he'd been holding. "But I need you in that meeting with me. You know more about this place than anyone. You've been here since the clinic opened. You know what's been happening around here, whereas I've just stepped into the job."

"I know, and I hate to let you down," she said, "but I

have no choice. Also—" she pushed the door closed behind her and approached his desk "—I have some information about Dr. Richie. And it's not good news."

He went still. The springs in Riley's chair creaked when he sat up straight, waiting.

"I was approached by Detective O'Callahan. He told me he was suspicious of Dr. Richie. I'd have told you about this sooner, but I didn't want to spread mere rumor. I told the detective I needed proof. Well, after doing some background research, the detective discovered that, although Dr. Richie excelled in some areas of study during his college years, he didn't do so well in chemistry. Detective O'Callahan has offered hard proof."

Even as he took the manila folder Faye handed him, Riley thought of all those small bottles the staff at the clinic had been handing out to clients right and left. A topical weight-loss oil, NoWait had been the invention of Dr. Richard Strong, the man who had been Chief of Staff of the clinic until a woman proclaiming to be his ex-wife had disrupted his standing-room-only seminar with loud and angry accusations that had caused him to run for the high hills. Dr. Richie—as the famous health guru was known by everyone in the Pacific Northwest—hadn't been seen in the clinic since.

The commotion had taken place a week ago, and although Riley hadn't been around to witness the incident, it had everyone abuzz, clients and staff alike, and he'd heard the story several times over. But he was doing all he could to suppress gossip. Riley had been shoved into this job with orders to smooth over the workings of the clinic and avoid scandal.

He whistled, low and long. "If the public discovers that Dr. Strong wasn't much of a chemist," he said, "yet he had our backing when he introduced that oil, there could be big trouble for the clinic. We've got to pull NoWait. We need to stop using it. Today."

Faye nodded. "I was hoping you'd say that."

"If the newspapers pick up the story about how that stuff is affecting our clients, it could ruin the clinic's reputation," Riley said.

"We've got to keep that from happening."

He unwittingly tapped the tip of his pen against the heel of his hand. "Granted, NoWait is a homeopathic treatment. It's topical, dab a bit on the skin. What can it harm? And Dr. Richie's papers only list natural ingredients. I've read them. I can't imagine NoWait being anything but harmless."

"It has seemed to help our clients lose weight," Faye said. "But everyone has also been acting rather…peculiar."

Peculiar wasn't the half of it, Riley silently surmised. The first day or so on the job, he'd been too busy to notice. But he'd quickly realized that the people in the clinic seemed more frisky than normal. And he didn't mean *frisky* as in lighthearted and playful, either. These people were downright lascivious.

"We can't automatically blame NoWait for this…odd behavior," he hurried to say. "Not without testing."

"That's true," Faye said. "Exercise does produce high amounts of endorphins to be released in the body. Endorphins that induce a 'feel good' effect. That could account for the behavior."

The higher-ups wanted this situation handled with kid gloves. They wouldn't be happy hearing that Riley and Faye wanted to yank NoWait from use. The clients loved the product. For more reasons than one.

"Or it could be," he said, "that everyone is experiencing the high of self-esteem produced by shedding those pounds and firming up, and that's why they're feeling amorous. A general, all-around dose of confidence might do it."

"Maybe," Faye murmured. But she clearly didn't believe it.

"Look, you need to be at that meeting," he told her firmly. "You've got the inside scoop on Richard Strong. You have that evidence. You need to make our case about the NoWait. I'll take the client off your hands."

"I can't let you do that. You're the boss around here now. The director. And besides that—"

"All I have to do is go over the nutrition booklet with her, right? I'll meet you over at the hospital just as soon as I finish with the woman, okay?" Riley could tell she was about to argue. "Listen, I can't have the meeting with hospital administration without you. But you can start it without me. I have every confidence in you."

The tension in her expression eased. "You'll come right over?"

Riley assured her he would.

She plucked a file from the top of the small stack she carried and handed it to him. "Her name's Catherine Houston. She's twenty-six and in good health. She's in conference room three. She's due at the gym after her nutrition orientation. Oh, and you should probably know..." Faye paused long enough to pinch her bottom lip between her teeth. "I think she's wealthy. Definitely upper crust. She purchased the whole line of vitamins, and some other supplements, too. And she bought several of the books we have for sale. She could be good for the clinic. So be nice to her."

Riley's mouth twisted. Rich, self-important people he could do without.

"Now, don't look like that," Faye chided. "It's not like she's arrogant or anything. Just the opposite, in fact. She's really personable. Very nice. I like her. I just thought we should be nice—"

"We're nice to everybody."

A groan rumbled from the back of her throat and she frowned. "Oh, forget I said anything. You're absolutely right." She waved her free hand in the air. "I'm just trying to think of anything and everything that will help us overcome the mess that Dr. Richie left us in. This whole thing has got me inside out and I'm not thinking clearly."

That was easy to believe. Her effusive remorse confirmed she was professional to the nth degree, and Riley knew that commenting on a client's affluence was atypical for her. Obviously, the situation had her stressed to the max. It had everyone stressed.

"I wish Dr. Richie would show his face," Faye muttered. "Sure would make my life easier."

"Everything's going to be okay," he assured her. "Go on over to the hospital and I'll get to the meeting just as soon as I can."

Alone in his office, he stared at the plain manila file in his hand and stifled a sigh.

Definitely upper crust.

Great. Just what he needed. A pretentious little rich girl.

He knew the type. Women who thought they were above people like him. What made it all the worse was that he knew it was true.

Faye had been adamant that this woman was friendly, but that wouldn't keep him from feeling second-rate. His mouth cocked cynically and he snatched up his lab coat.

Well, better to get the session over with, he thought,

pulling the door of his office closed behind him and making his way down the hall.

The door of the conference room was open, but the shapely blonde had her back to the door so Riley tapped to get her attention. She swung around to greet him, her shoulder-length hair swinging, her lush, shiny lips smiling to reveal two rows of perfect, pearly teeth. Her flawless skin glowed. And he imagined the silky feel of it beneath his fingertips.

Something strange twanged in his gut. The muscles there went tight as a knot. And his throat… It went so dry he felt as if he'd swallowed a mouthful of powder. The greeting he'd formed in his head refused to roll off his tongue.

Immediately, mild confusion knitted the woman's smooth brow.

"Is everything all right?" she asked.

Her voice had an exotic, Mediterranean lilt that triggered a reaction stemming from the most primitive part of his brain. The skin on the back of his neck quivered, and the urge to ask her to repeat herself welled up in him fiercely. Not because he hadn't heard her question. No, it wasn't that at all.

She blinked, thick, tawny lashes brushing against milky skin. "Dr. Lassen set me up with Sally Henderson, the nutritionist. Dr. Lassen said she'd try to stop by, too."

"Sally's out sick." Riley moved to the oak table and set the file on it. "And Dr. Lassen was called to a meeting. It was unavoidable. Have a seat and we can go over this information."

As greetings went, his had probably been too abrupt and not nearly friendly enough, but he seemed to be fighting his way out of a strange fog at the moment.

When she remained by the window on the far side of the room, Riley asked, "You *are* Catherine Houston?"

"Yes." She tucked a strand of wavy hair behind her ear, but only advanced a step or two closer to the table.

Her hesitation surprised him. Usually, women of her ilk were confident and assertive. He waited for her to finally reach him, and then he pulled out a chair for himself, hoping she'd follow suit. Opening the file Faye had given him, Riley found the booklet and thrust it toward her.

"Read this over," he instructed. "And I'll answer any questions you have."

She turned the booklet over in her hand, looked at the front and back cover. Then she flipped through the pages. A quick, unexpected grin played at the corners of her mouth, and Riley felt his belly go taut once again.

"I have to read this?" Her cute nose wrinkled.

"There is only one good—knowledge—and one evil—ignorance."

"Socrates."

"That's right," Riley said. "He was a smart man."

"Yes, but even Socrates would balk at swallowing all this in one sitting. Eighty-six pages?" she observed, glancing down at the last page. When she looked up at him, her eyes gleamed mischievously. "I don't mind reading. I'm just surprised you've got that kind of time on your hands to sit there while I do."

If she'd felt at all uncertain before, she'd certainly made a rapid recovery.

Good and truly put in his place, Riley said, "Yes, well...I didn't realize... Maybe we should just touch on the high points."

She laughed, and he felt the enticing notes slowly tumble down each vertebra of his backbone. His spine arched slightly, and he rested his elbow on the top of the conference table, liking the unexpected calmness that washed over him.

"There in the introduction—" he indicated the booklet in front of her and she flipped to the appropriate page "—you'll see that there are four basic nutrients: water, carbohydrates, proteins and fats. They're referred to as the building blocks of a good diet."

Her head was bent, her attention directed at the printed words. Riley couldn't help but notice how the sunlight streaming through the window glinted off her hair, igniting it like golden fire. She looked like an entrancing goddess.

"Good nutrition," he espoused verbatim from what he'd memorized since taking over as director, "is the foundation of good health."

He let his gaze rove over her profile, along her high cheekbone, down her pert nose and the curve of her jawline.

"Choosing the healthiest forms of those four basic nutrients," he continued, "and consuming them in the correct balance—" he took an instant to inhale the soft flowery scent of her "—will enable your body to function at its optimal level."

Catherine Houston roused something in him. Something deep. Something basic. It was almost as if she were luring him—in a way he hadn't been lured in a very long time.

Like a blaring horn, the dangerous thought snapped Riley out of the bizarre trance that had nearly ensnared him. He sat up straight, and with conscious effort, folded his hands into his lap.

Obviously he found the woman attractive. There was really nothing he could do about that. She was a beautiful woman. He was a red-blooded man. Physiologically, that was all it took.

She chose that moment to tip her head to the side and glance up at him. The smile she flashed beaned him like a two-by-four between the eyes, and his breath left him in a rush.

"Food is necessary," he blurted.

Her smile magnified, and so did his internal reaction.

"What I meant to say is that good nutrition is necessary." He slid his chair several inches from the table. "Look," he told her, his tone sharper than he intended, "the information you have there in that booklet is self-explanatory. It'll provide you with everything you need to know about nutrition and how what you eat affects your health. Read it at your convenience. If you have any questions, I'm sure Dr. Lassen would be happy to schedule another session with you."

What poor business practice! Faye would be upset with him, for sure. But he needed to get away from Catherine Houston. She was short-circuiting his brainwaves and turning him into a blubbering idiot.

Her sexy mouth parted, her surprise apparent, and her full bottom lip became the all-encompassing focal point of his concentration. His gaze skittered across it, and he imagined slowly tracing the outline of the smooth, dusky skin, first with a soft caress of his thumb, then with moist strokes of his tongue.

He stood, his thigh hitting one corner of the booklet that overhung the table and sending it shooting a good foot toward the center of the table. He cleared his throat and raked his fingers through his hair.

"Are you all right?"

What was that accent? he wondered. Italian? Greek?

Riley patted his breast pocket with a shaky hand, and immediately wondered what the hell he was looking for. "Fine," he said. "I'm fine. Like I said, read the book. And I'm sure Dr. Lassen will make herself available to you. She'd have been here today, but she was called to a meeting. And Sally's out sick."

"Yes," Catherine replied quietly. "You said that."

Great! As if uncalled-for rudeness weren't enough, now he was looking downright dopey. The woman *was* turning him into a blubbering idiot!

"Of course, I did. I was just…" He nodded, letting the rest of the thought fade because he had no idea what the hell the rest of the thought was. He was just what? So preoccupied with this woman's physical attributes that he'd lost track of what he had and hadn't said? "Well, if there's nothing else, I'll point the way to the gym. I'm sure you can find it. You don't seem directionally challenged."

Directionally challenged? Where was his brain coming up with this crap?

"There's a trainer wait—"

"Just a moment, please."

Riley went silent. There was sudden authority in her voice he hadn't heard before. He was just glad she'd said something that made him shut the hell up.

"I've been talking to some of the other clients," she said. "They told me about a weight-loss aid that the clinic offers."

"You want to lose weight?" He couldn't keep the incredulity out of his query. It was really none of his business why she'd come to the clinic, and humiliating the clients with discourteously toned questions was a worse business practice than asking them to reschedule appointments. But…

Why on earth would she think she needed to lose weight?

Her cheeks tinged pink. "I've got these nagging five pounds."

This was a prime example of why this job was going to send him round the bend. Helping to make perfect bodies even more perfect wasn't his idea of practicing medicine.

"So buy bigger trousers."

As soon as the words rolled off his tongue, Riley knew he'd made a terrible mistake.

But Catherine Houston didn't tell him off as he expected. Even though she probably had every right to. However, she didn't even seem insulted by his blunder. She remained amazingly composed.

No negative emotion tainted either her tone or her expression as she said, "Since buying bigger trousers isn't an option for my next shopping excursion, I'd like to ask you about NoWait." She paused, but not long enough for him to respond. "Everyone I've talked to just raves about the product. I've heard that it's all-natural. Can you tell me about it? What's it made of? How does it work? And how can I get my hands on a bottle?"

Riley pushed back the open facings of his lab coat and tucked his fists into his pockets. "I'm sorry to say the clinic isn't endorsing NoWait at the moment. That could change, of course. And if it does, we'll let you know. But—"

"Oh." Her smile waned. "I'd heard such amazing things about it, though. I was told a dab of the oil behind the ears melts off the pounds."

That was only one effect, unfortunately, Riley thought. The other one was a bit kinkier.

The decision to pull the oil made good sense. The change in the behavior of those who had been using No-

Wait was blatant. If word got out that the clinic was promoting a product that had people feeling uninhibited and spontaneously sexual, it could result in some very bad press for the clinic, and in this litigious day and age it could also mean lawsuits galore.

The silence grew awkward, and he realized she was waiting for more information. Well, she wouldn't get it from him.

"Another way to accomplish your goal," he said, "is by working out at our exercise facility." Proud of his smooth transition, he continued, "The gym is on the second floor. Take the elevator at the end of the hall. You can't miss it."

From the look on her face, he could tell she recognized the dismissal for what it was. Her silky blond hair fell over her shoulder as she shifted to pick up the booklet from the table. She took her time sliding out of her chair, the muscles in her shapely legs tensing, long and lean.

Riley didn't want to look, but he couldn't help himself.

Placing her hands on the padded armrests, she raised up to her full height. She had excellent posture, he noticed, his gaze skimming along the flare of her hips, her trim waist, the lush curve of her breasts. His tongue stuck to the roof of his cottony mouth. He couldn't swallow.

The woman was a knockout.

Her sapphire eyes flashed. "I want to thank you for the time you've spent with me today. You've been very helpful."

She lied with the utter perfection of having been schooled in the art. If his cheek muscles hadn't been paralyzed by her mere presence, he just might have smiled.

When she took a step toward him, the light scent of sun-warmed flowers wafted in the still air of the conference room. His gut tensed, and he could almost feel the smoky tendrils of that enticing trance plucking at him, tempting him all over again.

Time to make an exit. Riley murmured, "Have a great evening."

The fact that it was only two in the afternoon wasn't lost on him, but it was too late to retract his valediction, as he'd already turned on his heel and scurried from the room like a frightened rabbit.

Oregon was a lush and beautiful state. Catherine had landed in LAX and chartered a small private plane to Portland. This city had been very lucky for her cousin Max. He'd found great happiness here. Was she hoping it would be lucky for her, too?

Sighing, she lifted her face up to the sunshine. The trainer she'd met in the gym had encouraged her to work hard. Then she'd whiled away the afternoon with a good, long steam, a massage and a warm shower. She felt like a new woman as she pushed open the glass doors and exited the clinic.

She'd told her father she needed time. That hadn't been a lie. She wished she had more than the two weeks he'd given her to get used to the idea of marrying a man she didn't love. She'd told her father she planned to shop for her trousseau. On that point she'd stretched the truth a bit, she feared. Shopping for a wedding she wanted nothing to do with wasn't high on her priority list.

She wasn't quite sure what she was looking for from this trip. But for right now, she simply wanted to forget about home, forget she was royal, forget all about her impending engagement, her looming nuptials. She wanted to be just like everyone else. Was that so much to ask?

"Dr. Lassen, hello!" Catherine was pleasantly surprised to meet the nutritionist in the outdoor breezeway between the hospital and the new health clinic. "It's a beautiful afternoon, isn't it?"

"Lovely." The doctor greeted her with a smile. "I'm awfully sorry I couldn't check in on you as I'd promised, Catherine."

"It's quite all right. I hope you don't mind my saying this, but you look awfully harried."

The woman nodded. "I just came out of a meeting. Many men. Much testosterone."

"Stressful, huh?" Catherine grinned. "Sounds like you need a break. I was just looking for a place to have a cup of tea. Want to join me?"

Dr. Lassen shifted her briefcase from one hand to the other. "I'd love to. And I'd kill for a muffin to go along with it. I worked right through lunch today and then I had to meet with hospital administration all afternoon."

"Let's find you something to eat, then," Catherine said.

"There's a coffee shop just around the corner."

They headed off along the crowded sidewalk.

"How did you make out today?" Dr. Lassen asked.

Humor had Catherine's mouth twitching. "Who was that man you sent to see me? The one who filled in for Sally."

"Dr. Riley Jacobs. He's the new director at the clinic," she said.

Dr. Riley Jacobs. His treatment of her had left Catherine feeling a bit put off. And surprised.

She'd read a great write-up about Portland's Healthy Living Clinic in the newspaper the very first day of her arrival. Apparently it was a friendly place, one that was extremely popular with the locals. Unlike some of the exclusive fitness centers that catered to the affluent sector of the population, this clinic was a facility where anyone and everyone could go to improve their health and well-being.

Since she'd decided to shed her royal status and become a run-of-the-mill tourist for a bit, Catherine had thought that the clinic could be the perfect place for her to meet people as well as lose a few extra pounds.

She'd toured the clinic with Faye Lassen yesterday and had arrived today feeling fired up about starting her fitness regimen…but the handsome Dr. Riley Jacobs had nearly snuffed out her flame.

"Why?" Faye frowned slightly. "What did he do?"

"Well," Catherine began, "I guess it's more what he didn't do."

Before she could explain further, they arrived at the coffee shop and spent a few moments being seated by the hostess. And then the waitress arrived with menus.

"I don't believe we need those," Catherine told the teen-ager. "We'd like two cups of tea, please. And a muffin for Dr. Lassen."

"Blueberry or low-fat bran?" the waitress asked the doctor.

Dr. Lassen chose the bran.

Once the teen walked away, Dr. Lassen planted both elbows on the tabletop. "Now that you've rescued me for a much-needed break, I think that makes us friends, don't you think? You have to call me Faye."

Catherine smiled. "I'll be happy to call you both. Faye and friend."

Faye reached for the napkin, shook it out and placed it in her lap. "Now let's get back to Dr. Jacobs and what it was he didn't do. He was supposed to go over the nutrition information with you, but if you have to ask his name, it seems he didn't even introduce himself."

"Oh, he attempted to go over the information," she assured Faye. "But something happened. He seemed to become…" Catherine searched for just the right word, but finally had to settle on one that didn't seem to her to be quite appropriate. "Befuddled."

Faye reached up and pushed her glasses higher on her nose. "I'd use a lot of words to describe Dr. Jacobs, but *befuddled* would never be one of them. He's extremely capable. Very intense. So much so that he can be a little grumpy at times."

"Bearish and brusque was the description I came up with." Catherine grinned. Once he'd left the conference room and she realized that her nose had gotten out of joint, she'd decided that no one—other than her father—had ever treated her so curtly before. She'd wanted to call after Dr. Jacobs and ask if he had any idea just who she was. However, she'd immediately chuckled to herself.

Of course, he hadn't had any idea who she was. And that was exactly how she wanted it.

The entire time she was working out in the gym, she'd thought about the incident, and she was actually pleased that the man had felt free enough to show his true colors. If he'd known her identity, he'd have probably been less candid.

She'd wanted to forget the problem she was facing and experience the regular, workaday world. And that was just what she was doing.

"Ah, so you did see his gruff side."

"Just a touch."

Faye sighed. "Sorry about that."

The waitress served their tea and Faye's muffin. Both

women thanked the girl before she went off to check on other customers.

"Don't apologize," Catherine said to Faye, automatically reaching for the string attached to the tea bag. "He didn't bother me. In fact, I may have deserved the terseness. I was pressing for information, you see. I'd heard about NoWait from some of the people I'd talked to before leaving the clinic yesterday. When he told me the oil wasn't being used any longer, I should have left well enough alone." She lifted one shoulder a fraction. "But I didn't."

Faye's mouth flattened. "Yes, we have pulled NoWait. For the time being, anyway. In fact, Dr. Jacobs is still in the meeting with hospital administration. He arrived after he'd met with you. It was his decision to stop using No-Wait. But I back him one hundred percent."

Catherine was disappointed all over again. From what she'd heard from the people in the gym that oil was like some kind of phenomenon. "That's too bad."

"It was causing some side effects that were…unexpected." Faye seemed to put extra effort into splitting her muffin in half.

The comment made Catherine curious, but her probing for information on NoWait had already gotten her into trouble once today so she let her questions go unasked. "Well, unexpected side effects can't be good."

Faye lifted her chin. "That's the consensus of hospital administration, too. But we're thinking of doing some testing. That's what Dr. Jacobs is up there discussing now." She nibbled the muffin and swallowed. "Now, back to your session with him. Did he answer your questions about a healthy diet? If not, I'm going to give him what for when I get back to the clinic."

"Oh, please, no." Catherine set the tea bag on the saucer. "Don't say anything to him. As I said, he did go over a little bit with me."

A very little bit.

She paused long enough to sip from the cup. "But then he got all flustered and started repeating himself." She tried not to smile. "He seemed to be a little confused with the time of day. He was tense about something, that much was clear." Absently, she picked up her spoon and swirled it in the hot liquid. "He actually ended up rushing out of the room."

"Hmmm." Faye's eyebrows arched. "That sure doesn't sound like him at all." Something in her gaze twinkled. "But the mere peculiarity of it does sound interesting, though."

After a moment, Catherine commented, "He doesn't smile much, does he?" Then she lapsed back into memories of her short time with him. Finally, she couldn't hold back her question any longer. "Is he married?"

Faye stirred a splash of cream into her tea. "Dr. Jacobs? No."

The cup warmed Catherine's fingers as she cradled it between both hands. "He's quite good-looking."

"Um-hmm," Faye agreed. She tipped her head a fraction. "You interested?"

"Let's put it this way, I like handsome men just as much as any other woman does." Catherine straightened the angle of the spoon sitting in her saucer. "I don't mind admitting that there's something about Dr. Jacobs that intrigues me...."

Ever since she'd turned twenty-one, she'd had a slew of men chosen for her—very wealthy, very appropriate, very boring and forgettable men. But there was nothing about Riley Jacobs that was forgettable. In fact, he had been on her mind all afternoon. What was it about him that attracted her?

Almost as if she'd heard the silent question that whispered through Catherine's head, Faye teasingly suggested, "Could it be the challenge?"

A mysterious and awesome sensation suddenly filled her...a sensation so delicious it had her wanting to curl her toes into the soles of her shoes.

"Could be," Catherine breathed. "It very well could be."

Two

Catherine sat in the exam room tapping her fingers against the side of the paper-covered mattress on which she sat. When she'd asked to make an appointment with Dr. Jacobs, she'd meant she merely wanted to talk to the man. However, the receptionist must have misunderstood and thought she needed medical assistance and had escorted her here.

Oh, well. It didn't matter to Catherine if she talked to Riley in his office or in an examination room. She only wanted to talk to him.

Although the walls were painted a peaceful shade of blue, the newness of everything lent a stark feel. She wondered if all doctors in America tended to their patients in such impersonal surroundings.

A robe had been draped on the mattress for her. But she hadn't touched it. Catherine couldn't imagine taking off her clothing and wrapping the flimsy fabric around her body.

She felt a sudden appreciation for the royal physician who was on call twenty-four hours a day, seven days a week for the von Husden family. Dr. Wallingford rushed to the palace to treat her father or her sisters or herself in the comfort of their own bedchambers whenever the need arose. However, house calls, as Americans would call them, were a thing of the past in this fast-paced, ultramodern society, she was sure.

Sitting on the exam table, Catherine felt her heart flutter. Her bout of nerves was caused by the brazenness of summoning Dr. Riley Jacobs, she knew. There wasn't a darn thing wrong with her. And she wondered how he would react to that. What he would say. How he would be. But the most interesting speculation of all was whether she could make him smile.

That was her sole goal in being here.

Normally, anywhere she went she was treated with the utmost respect. Everyone she met practically fell over themselves to supply her every whim. But Dr. Jacobs didn't know she was Princess Catherine von Husden. He'd had no idea when they'd met the day before yesterday that he'd been in the presence of royalty.

Royalty schmoyalty. What good was a gem-encrusted tiara, she wondered, if it kept you guessing whether people were treating you well simply because you were who you were, or because they truly wanted to be your friend?

She wanted Dr. Jacobs to be her friend. Heck, that wasn't the full truth. She wanted more from him than that. She'd come to Portland seeking a naughty adventure. This vacation she'd planned would be her one and only chance to experience the sparks that flashed between a man and a woman.

All she had to do was figure out how to make his sparks flash. Catherine chuckled at the thought.

However, instinct told her that if she was going to get anywhere with the good doctor, the first thing she had to do was make him smile.

Two short raps on the door had her lifting her gaze. Dr. Jacobs pushed his way into the small exam room, his brow marred with a frown.

"So where are you hurting? You strain a muscle in the gym?"

Nothing like being direct. He was so grumpy, it was kind of cute.

"Hello to you, too," she said.

Her bright greeting made him pause. He remained silent, just looking at her, and Catherine took full advantage of the quick second to give him a thorough once-over.

His eyes were a rich shade of brown with enticing flecks of amber. His eyelashes were thick. His hair—chestnut-brown with deep red highlights—was short and traditionally styled. She liked his clean-cut look. His smooth skin had an olive tone.

"When you were training to become a doctor," she quipped, "you must have missed the lesson on bedside manner."

The bedazzling smile she offered him had won over the Queen of England, herself. Surely it would charm him, too.

His frown faded, but his wide mouth didn't curl up at the ends as she had hoped it would. Well, she'd just have to try harder.

"Just trying to get down to business." He tossed the file onto the counter and reached for the stethoscope draped around his neck.

"I can't say I know a thing about being a doctor," she

began, "but I'd think part of the 'business' of treating people is garnering their trust. Putting them at ease so they'll feel comfortable enough to tell you about their problem."

His jaw went tight. Apparently he didn't take kindly to her friendly advice.

Feeling suddenly mischievous, she wondered just how far she could goad him until he caught on that he was being goaded.

"What would it hurt for you to have come into the room and greeted me with a happy hello?"

He dipped his chin just a bit. "Lady, I don't give anyone a happy hello."

That didn't surprise her in the least. "Well, maybe you should. And how about asking about my day? That might be nice."

The man looked about to implode, and Catherine could barely contain her laughter.

"Do you know," she continued, "that we met two days ago, sat down together and talked, and you never even introduced yourself. I didn't know your name until I asked Dr. Lassen. You're too tense, Dr. Jacobs. Too focused." She pinched her chin between her thumb and fingers, narrowing her gaze. "Do you think that's a problem you might need to work on?"

A storm brewed all around him.

"I'll have you know," he said, "that up until a week and a half ago, I was treating real patients with real problems. I didn't have time for happy hellos." Annoyance tightened the muscles in his face, making the angles sharper, more defined. "The people I treated were most often unconscious and completely helpless. There wasn't time for polite conversation."

Wow, she'd whipped him up into a real huff. She ought to be ashamed that she'd enjoyed doing it.

Curiosity had her wondering about the previous job he'd just described, but now wasn't the time to ask. She was too close to her goal of provoking him to his limit. She tilted her head and queried, "So you're saying I'm not real?"

She injected the question with a jesting tone, let the humor she felt twinkle in her eyes.

Finally realizing he was being purposely prodded, he shook his head. Then he looked down at the floor, chuckling.

The sound was rich and heady. Catherine liked it. A lot.

And when he lifted his gaze to hers, he was smiling.

Smiling.

A tingling heat permeated Catherine's entire body.

"No," he said softly. "I'm not saying that at all. You're perfectly real."

He draped his stethoscope back around his neck and laced his fingers together at his waist.

"You should smile more often," she told him.

He nodded. "You're probably right."

Silence hung between them, heavy and cumbersome. If she didn't know better, she'd have sworn that the temperature in the room rose several degrees.

Her grin was smug. "No probably about it. That smile suits you. Loosens up everything. The tenseness in your body—" without thought, her tone lowered an octave "—in our conversation...in the very air."

She did feel an easing of the strain in him, both physically and emotionally, and in their conversation. But the air remained dense. Deliciously thick. His irritation was no longer the culprit, she realized. What swirled around them now was something shadowy. Something both mysterious and exciting.

Catherine hoped he didn't intend to use that stethoscope to listen to her heart any time soon, because if he did, he couldn't miss the way it fluttered against her ribs.

"Okay, so maybe we need to start over." He offered her his hand. "Hello. My name is Dr. Riley Jacobs."

She slid her palm against his and curled her fingers around his hand. His skin was warm, his handshake firm.

"I'm Catherine Houston," she told him, pleased to play along. "My family calls me Cat. But I prefer Catherine."

"Catherine it is, then."

The handshake ended and she felt a twinge of disappointment.

"And how are you today?" He measured each word carefully.

"Much better now."

Much better! she thought.

"So what brings you in to see me today? Did you strain a muscle? Are you sore from overexertion?"

In a sudden quandary, Catherine remained silent. He was being pleasant now, sure. But as soon as she told him there was nothing wrong with her, he'd probably be peeved that she'd wasted his time.

"Well," she started out haltingly, "I don't really have a physical injury."

"Oh?" Uncertainty clouded his eyes, yet at the same time curiosity had his brows arching the tiniest bit.

"I don't know if you're aware," she said, "but I'm a visitor to Portland. I came here because my cousin visited the city not too long ago and he just raved about the place."

Her cousin Max had met his wife here in Oregon. And he'd defied convention completely when he'd married Ivy Crosby, too.

"So I thought I'd escape from…everything—" The

words snagged in her throat and she gave a small cough. She needed to be careful or she was going to give away her secret. "I wanted to see what kind of fun I could find in Portland," she finished.

"And what kind of fun have you found?"

He was giving tolerance and patience a valiant effort, but she could tell this small talk was driving him nuts.

She couldn't help but observe, "You're really a workaholic, aren't you?"

Her question took him aback. There was defensiveness in his tone when he said, "I don't know that I'd say that."

Catherine ignored him. "You must have a reputation of working hard. How else could you land the top job at a place like this? I mean, look at you. You're champing at the bit to do something—analyze my symptoms, diagnose my problem—so you can move on to the next crisis."

His rigid shoulders relaxed and he actually laughed.

She'd found him appealing before, but this laid-back manner of his enthralled her.

"Sounds like I'm the one being diagnosed here. But I don't mind reminding you that you're the one who made this appointment. With me. The doctor. The one wearing the white coat and the stethoscope. So if we can just stick to the topic at hand…" He tossed her a pointed look.

Chagrin had her averting her gaze, and she shifted her hips until the edge of exam table pressed against the backs of her knees.

"You were explaining this nonphysical problem of yours," he prompted.

"I was." Bolstering herself with a deep breath, she said, "The people I've met here at the clinic's gym are great, but everyone seems so busy with work or their families. No one seems to have time for a new friend. I was able to enjoy a cup of tea with Dr. Lassen. But I've been eating dinner alone every night. I've been doing a little sight-seeing, but—" she sighed dramatically "—it's just not the same when you're all on your own."

With each sentence she spoke the crease between his eyebrows cut deeper into his forehead.

"Are you trying to tell me that you're suffering from loneliness?"

"Well, you don't have to say it like that." She tucked her arms across her chest and informed him, "It's a perfectly legitimate ailment."

Even though humor continued to sparkle in his chocolate eyes, he did a great job of mustering up some solemnity. "Of course it is."

She forced her spine to straighten. "So it's official? I've been diagnosed?" Without waiting for him to answer her silly questions, she barreled ahead. "Then what I'd like you to do is write me a prescription. For some company. For some conversation." She thought a moment and then boldly announced, "I think a sight-seeing tour of Portland would be nice. Coffee and dessert would be great. Oh, and dinner, too. Not necessarily in that order, of course."

He looked quite stunned. She decided to go in for the kill before he could regain his wits.

"And if you're truly dedicated to your profession," she said, "you'll volunteer to be my guide for the evening."

Now he had that deer-caught-in-headlights expression, and it was all Catherine could do not to laugh.

"Y-you want a date?"

She flashed a huge grin at him, purposefully mistaking his question. "I'd love a date, thank you. I accept your invitation, Dr. Jacobs."

* * *

Later that same day, Riley sat at his desk and listened as Carrie Martin explained her story.

"I had no idea who that Dr. Richie person was up there in front of that crowd."

The woman's eyes had taken on a haunted look, and sympathy rose up in Riley. Obviously, Carrie was reliving that awful confrontation she'd initiated during Dr. Richie's last seminar before he'd disappeared. Up until now, he'd only heard rumor and innuendo, and he'd squelched that as quickly as he could, thinking that was best for the clinic and its reputation. But this woman had been deeply affected by the ugly incident that she, herself, had admittedly been the center of.

"I mean, he resembled the man I'd married years ago in Florida," she continued, "but that Dr. Richie person strutting back and forth and tossing out all that overly dramatized gibberish was just too…" Her sentence trailed off and she shook her head.

Riley had never personally met Richard Strong, but having inherited the job of cleaning up the man's mess here at the clinic—and the potential problems that could ensue—Riley had certainly learned a great deal of secondhand information about the man. Some people loved him, saw him as charismatic. He apparently had a way of garnering people's trust. And Riley had heard it said that the man could sell ice cubes in Antarctica. And the suits in Administration had loved that "salesman" aspect of Dr. Richie's personality. Plus, when he'd accepted the job of running the clinic, the famous guru of the Northwest had brought quite a fan following along with him.

But there were plenty of people who had their doubts about the man and his tactics.

"I just can't believe what he's done," Carrie continued, amazement filling her tone to the brim. "What kind of person is he that he felt he needed to change his name?"

Riley perked up. "He changed his name?"

"Yes," Carrie said. "He was born Strokudnowski. Richard Strokudnowski."

A difficult name to spell, Riley decided as he attempted to jot it down.

"Well, there's really nothing wrong with a name change," he told her. "Lots of people do it." Riley hoped he didn't offend her. He only meant to offer another view. "Especially prominent people. Stars and the like. They want to be called something that makes an impact, something that's easy to remember. *Strong* is much easier to remember than *Strow…Strew…*" His eyes grew wide when he realized that Richard Strong's given name had slipped right out of his brain.

"Strokudnowski." Her mouth quirked. "I see what you mean."

"And surely you know," he went on, "that Dr. Richie has been making a name for himself in the fitness world for some time now."

"I've recently discovered his fame." She winced as she asked, "But Dr. Richie? It sounds so lame."

Riley shrugged. He thought the name sounded pretty silly, too, and wanted to shake his head every time he was forced to say it, but who knew how the Dr. Richie phenomenon got started?

"Sometimes a person grows larger than life," he suggested, "and the fans are the ones who do the choosing."

Her expression told him she hadn't thought of that possibility before this moment.

"Dr. Jacobs, I need to find him." She scooted to the edge

of the seat. "I feel so bad about what I did, about what I said in that seminar. I need him to know that. Can you tell me where he's gone? Did he move out of the state? Did he take a job at another clinic?"

"I'm sorry." He shook his head, truly empathizing with the woman. "I don't know where he is. Actually, we're looking for him, too."

Her eyes grow round. "Is he in trouble? Did I—"

"He's not in trouble," he assured her. "We've decided to do some testing on his weight-loss treatment."

"NoWait."

Riley nodded.

"I was asked to go give back my bottle," she said.

Again, he nodded. "We're hoping to collect as much of it as we can."

"I'm relieved."

Her response startled him into silence. Most of the clinic's clients were upset about having to surrender their No-Wait.

"Dr. Jacobs," she said in a lower tone, "I've been visiting the clinic for weeks now. Since that oil was introduced, people around here have been acting like a bunch of horny toads ready to dry-hump anything that stands still long enough." Her jaw dropped open and the color drained from her face. "I can't believe I said that to a perfect stranger. I tend to let down my guard with people way too quick. Please forgive me."

Riley cleared his throat, quashing his urge to chuckle, and attempted to remain unruffled. "It's quite all right. This is an, uh, unusual situation we find ourselves in. We're all a little off-kilter." He rushed to get the conversation back to the testing. "There's quite a bit of money being made today in specialty medicines meant to treat sexual disorders. If—and that's a big if—Richard Strong has come up with a topical treatment made of natural ingredients, the results could be far reaching. But testing needs to be done. We're going to get it started, but we'd like Dr. Richie to head up the effort."

Once she'd regained her composure, Carrie said, "I feel I really need to be frank here. The man I married wasn't—" She stopped, uncertainty shadowing her face. Then she tried again. "Although the Richard I attended college with was very caring and wanted very much to help people, there was no way I'd allow him to prepare any kind of remedy for me. He wasn't a detail-oriented person, if you know what I mean, and formulating substances wasn't one of his strongest talents."

Ah, Riley thought, so the man's less-than-scholarly reputation wasn't just a myth.

"Don't worry," Riley assured her. "He'd have chemists and lab assistances at his disposal. However, judging from the amorous behavior we've witnessed, it seems he's on to something significant."

Carrie took a deep breath. "So you're trying to find him?"

"Very discreetly. We know he's still in town. He's been seen. But he's not answering his phone or returning calls. The staff here has to be very careful. It's not like he's missing, or in danger. He has a right not to be found if that's what he wants."

The woman nodded. "But I can look for him, right? I won't be breaking any laws if I look for him myself?"

"I don't believe so." He flattened his palms out on the desktop. "If you do find him, please have him come to see us. Or tell him at least to call."

Regret rounded her shoulders, and she clutched the handbag on her lap. "The way he left the conference room that day," she said, "I'm sure he's feeling very embarrassed."

Riley agreed but he didn't allow himself to nod. He didn't want to make her feel any worse than she already did.

"Dr. Jacobs, was there ever a time when you wished you could relive a day in your life? Just one day? Just one hour? Heck, I'd take reliving just one minute. Wouldn't it be nice if we could reach out and snatch back the words we say that hurt someone else?"

"Everyone has had that wish at one time or another."

But Carrie hadn't heard him. He could tell. She was too wrapped up in her misery.

She stared, unseeing, at a spot just over his left shoulder as she whispered, "What I wouldn't give to be able to take it all back."

Riley walked through the plush lobby with Catherine on his arm, still dumbfounded that one, he'd allowed himself to be bamboozled into a date, and two, that the bamboozler was the innocent-looking yet heart-stoppingly gorgeous woman at his side.

He'd spent the whole afternoon trying to figure out just how she'd gotten him to agree to take her to dinner. She hadn't threatened or harassed. She hadn't even pestered him, really. She'd lulled him into some sort of trancelike state—the same turmoil that had frightened the bejesus out of him the first time they'd met—and then she'd swooped in to exploit his weakened condition.

Riley prayed to high heaven that she hadn't really realized he'd been suffering with a helpless fragility due to his oh-too-physical reaction to her, and that he'd merely agreed to treat the outlandish illness she'd labeled as lonesomeness by taking her out on the town.

But he wasn't certain the town of Portland was ready for the likes of Catherine Houston. He cut her a quick sidelong glance.

She was a stunner. The black dress she wore clung to the curves of her luscious body. Her stiletto heels accentuated about a mile's worth of firm and shapely legs. She was enough to make a man salivate.

"So what do you have planned?"

Her voice sounded like a soft caress.

Normally well grounded in realism, Riley was not a fanciful thinker. Relating her question to a soft touch was out-of-character for him. But even that realization didn't keep the hair on his arms from standing on end. Riley shook his head and inhaled a lungful of mind-clearing oxygen.

"It's a surprise," he told her, holding open the heavy glass door for her. "We still have some daylight left. I have something I want to show you. One of my favorite places. We won't get to stay long because they close at six. But you'll get to experience a little of it, at least."

Portland's Classical Chinese Garden was a walled oasis. Located smack-dab in the center of "old town," the gardens encompassed a full block of serpentine walkways, open colonnades and Asian architecture. The landscape was meticulously arranged with rare and unusual plants, mosaic stone paths and a small bridged lake.

Delight shined from Catherine's eyes when they entered, and Riley told her, "Believe it or not, this used to be a parking lot. Back in the eighties, Portland became a sister city with Suzhou, China. Not long after, this land was donated and construction began on the garden."

For several long moments they walked in silence, simply enjoying the sights, sounds and scents of nature.

Closing her eyes, she tipped up her chin and inhaled.

"Mmmm," she murmured. "I just love jasmine. Always have."

Riley let his gaze trail down the long length of her milky throat. He envisioned himself pressing his nose to her heated, silky skin.

Realization suddenly struck. "That's what you smell like. Jasmine."

Her blue eyes sparked with appreciation, and warmth rushed to his face. He had no idea why he felt embarrassed over his remark. This woman made him react in the most peculiar ways.

"I—I couldn't place the flowery scent in your perfume before," he stammered. "But now I know. It's jasmine."

Her wide mouth curled softly. Deliciously. He got the distinct sense that she was grateful he'd noticed. The expression on her lovely face caused a repositioning of the warmth that had been in his face and neck, and the heat raced right to the pit of his gut.

"A French perfumery makes this scent just for me," she said, and as soon as the words slipped from her lips, she looked annoyed.

"What is it?"

One wavy blond tress fell over her shoulder when she shook her head. "It's nothing," she told him.

"Of course it's something. Your brow is knitted tighter than the wool scarf my mother sent me for my birthday." He stopped, deciding not to take another step on the stone pathway until she answered his question.

She halted a couple steps ahead and then had to turn to face him. Evidently realizing she'd have to confess, she shrugged. "It's just that I'm not a good liar."

He chuckled. "And that's a bad thing because…?"

"Well, I wanted to spend my time in Portland as any

other average, ordinary woman." Irony tightened one corner of her mouth. "But average, ordinary women don't have perfume specially blended in France, do they?"

He wasn't sure how he felt about her query. But one thing was clear. Faye had been correct; Catherine was a cut above. Just how far above, he had no idea.

"Catherine," he began, "even without your small slipup, there's no way that I'd ever think you were average. There's not one thing about you that's ordinary."

Her countenance only became more glum and that made him chuckle out loud. But he quickly checked himself. People visiting the gardens liked the quiet. It was what they came here for.

"Stop that frowning," he ordered. "Sticking out in a sea of standard isn't a bad thing, Catherine. Some people can't help it. And you're one of them."

Her face brightened a little. "If anyone ever asks me, I'll just have to say that, no matter how grumpy the good doctor can be, he certainly can give nice compliments."

He waved off her teasing. They started off down the path, and the heel of Catherine's shoe caught on the stones. She lurched forward. Riley caught her by the upper arm and automatically drew her securely against his chest.

He couldn't tell if the warm scent of jasmine in the air was coming from the flowers nearby or from her skin. Her golden hair brushed his cheek like the feathers of an angel's wing.

"I'm sorry. These shoes aren't very good on this uneven ground." He supported her while she lifted one knee and bent to rub her ankle.

"I'm the one who should be sorry," he told her. "I should have known better than to bring you—"

"Stop," she insisted, lowering her foot back to the ground. "I'm fine. But can we sit for few minutes?"

"Of course."

He led her to a nearby pavilion and they sat on the bench. A waterfall gurgled just behind them, and peace seemed to permeate the very air.

"This place is just wonderful," Catherine breathed.

"I come here often. I enjoy trying to figure out the meaning behind the poetry couplets that are scattered throughout the garden. And I like the fact that each artistic effect in the garden has an important symbolic meaning."

She nodded. "Now I get it."

"Get what?"

"When we first arrived," she said, "I couldn't understand why a man like you would even know about a place like this."

He didn't understand. "A man like me?" He lifted one hand, palm up. "A place like this?"

"You have to admit that you and this garden are, well, opposites. Close your eyes a second and feel it. This place is serene and stress-free, content to simply exist. Sure, I hardly know you, but from what I've witnessed, you're none of those things."

Her tongue skipped across her dusky lips, and Riley had to force himself not to stare.

"But the poetry and the symbolism," she continued, "make this a thinking man's garden, now don't they?"

Riley felt discomfited. He wasn't sure he liked being analyzed. She'd done the same thing earlier today, evaluated his character.

"You don't have to answer." She reached up and tucked her hair behind her ear. "I didn't mean to make you uncomfortable."

Catherine crossed her long, sexy legs, then leaned forward, resting her forearm on her knee. She looked down at the ground, and then tipped up her chin to gaze into his face. Like a magnet, her creamy cleavage drew his gaze.

Something amazing gathered in those deep blue eyes of hers. And just as amazing were the mysterious tendrils that seemed to sprout from the very ground and climb along his legs, grappling and grasping and plucking at him.

Touch her. Kiss her. Taste her.

The phantom whisper seemed to come from nowhere. And everywhere. Every leaf, every drop of water, every pebble and rock vibrated with a wraithlike energy that called him to act.

The urge to reach out and stroke the graceful line of her jaw nearly overpowered him.

Riley's mouth went desert-dry, and he cleared his throat with a small cough.

"We should go," he told her. He stood, before the strange spell completely smothered all his good and logical sense. "I have other places for you to see, other things for us to do. This is a tour, remember."

Determination resided on her pretty face, hinting that she was quite happy with the "thing" they were doing right now. But he pushed the issue by holding out his hand to her.

And after exhaling a quick, regretful sigh, she took it.

Three

Dusk was falling as he headed out of the city on Highway 29. Riley didn't have to go far. Satisfaction took root in him when, rounding a slight bend in the road, he heard Catherine's sharp intake of breath.

"Beautiful," she whispered.

"That's Mount Hood." He pulled to the shoulder and cut the engine. "In just a minute, you'll see why this is called Sunset Highway."

The sun hung low on the horizon, and the alpenglow it cast on the snow-covered cliff face was a pink so deep that they both went speechless for several long moments. They sat in silence. The color intensified, diffusing from pink to mauve, and from mauve to a rich magenta. Once the sun had disappeared altogether, the icy precipice radiated an electric midnight blue.

Finally, twilight darkened the sky, and the brightest of

the stars became visible and twinkled overhead. The air in the car was still and quiet. Catherine's jasmine scent caressed each breath Riley took. But then his breath caught in his throat when he heard the erotic sound of fabric against leather as she shifted on the seat.

"Wow." She turned to face him, speaking softly, almost reverently. "At first I was disappointed that we were leaving the city. But that was…amazing. Thank you for bringing me out here to see it."

"You're welcome." Riley turned the key and the engine roared to life. "We need to make a beeline back to Portland," he told her, checking to see that the roadway was clear before making a tight U-turn. "I hope we don't hit any traffic because we've got dinner reservations in twenty minutes. I hope you like Italian."

"I love Italian."

During the drive back to Portland, they chatted about Catherine's workout routine, and Riley was pleased to hear that she found the clinic staff helpful and friendly.

He couldn't help but notice that her voice held a spark that lifted his spirits, a playfulness that he found enticing. This woman allured him, that was undeniable.

As it turned out, finding a parking spot was their biggest problem. They'd had to circle the block three times before finding an available space. Riley took Catherine's arm so they could hurry down the street to the restaurant. They arrived with barely a minute to spare. They were out of breath and grinning as they were seated at their table.

He ordered wine, and after he went through the tasting ritual, the waiter filled their glasses and left them alone to look over the menu.

"The antipasto is delicious," he suggested.

Her pert nose wrinkled. "But the cheese and the olives

and the pepperoni." She gave a slight shake of her head. "Lots of calories. I think I'll have a green salad."

His eye traveled down the list of entrees. "I've had the shrimp with linguini," he told her. "It's out of this world."

"Shrimp are full of cholesterol."

He arched his brows a fraction, but remained silent.

"I never knew that," she said, "until I read about it in the clinic's nutrition book."

Spying another of his favorites, he offered, "The ravioli with classic Bolognese is delicious. They make the ravioli by hand right back there in the kitchen."

"Heavy cream, pancetta," she read the ingredients aloud from the menu description. She looked up at him. "It's all so fattening."

Frustration got the better of him. "But that's what makes it so good."

Her mouth screwed up, and she muttered, "Tell me about it."

"Catherine, splurging once in a while isn't going to kill you."

She sighed. "You've never had a weight problem, have you?"

"No, I haven't. And I seriously doubt that you ever have, either. I'll go even farther out on the limb and say that about eighty percent of the people who visit the clinic don't have any real weight problems. The biggest problem, I think, is in their heads. In their perceptions of themselves."

At that moment, the waiter arrived to take their order. With his feathers duly ruffled, Riley chose the antipasto and the shrimp linguini. And when it came time for dessert, he intended to order something rich and chocolaty, too.

"I'd like the house salad," Catherine told the waiter. "Dressing on the side, please. And I'll have the spaghetti marinara with just a shaving or two of parmesan."

"I'll be right back with your salads." The waiter took their menus and retreated to the kitchen.

Riley picked up his glass and sipped his wine.

Catherine settled back in her chair and crossed her arms. "I see that I need to set you straight on a thing or two. I did have a problem with my weight when I was a child. I was a roly-poly little girl. And lonely, as well.

"I'm surprised that you'd demean the people who seek help from your clinic by diminishing the trouble they're having with self-control and with motivating themselves to exercise. Granted, being overweight isn't imminently life-threatening. But it leads to terrible health problems. You're a doctor. You know that. You have to know that those—"

"Hey, hold on." He leaned toward her, setting down his glass on the table. "I was only trying to offer you a compliment. To me, you look fit."

Hell, she looked more than merely fit. She was enough to make a man break every promise he'd ever made.

"To me," he continued, "most of the people coming to the clinic look to be in perfect health." He shrugged. "Yes, we do have clients who are overweight. Some are even obese. But for the most part, I can easily see the clinic turning into another trendy place where people come to make their perfect bodies even more perfect."

He was simply attempting to explain his thoughts on the matter, but it was clear he'd only irritated her further.

"It's called keeping in shape. I'm surprised that you have so little compassion for those of us who really have to work at it."

"I have plenty of compassion," he assured her. He sighed, toying absently with one corner of the pristine white linen napkin neatly folded in front of him. "I have to admit that I never, in my wildest imaginings, expected to be managing things at a health clinic."

"Ah, so your blasé attitude toward those with weight problems has less to do with the people who come to the clinic and more to do with you?"

He picked up his glass and took another swallow. "Calling me blasé is a little harsh. Let's just say that, with all the intensive and extensive training I've had, I expected to be treating gunshot wounds and heart attacks, not checking triglycerides and prescribing jumping jacks."

The annoyance that had tightened her jaw muscles waned and some unreadable emotion cast shadows in her sparkling blue eyes. Curiosity, maybe? He couldn't be sure. But the waiter arrived with their salads and he spent a few moments filling their water goblets and grinding fresh black pepper for them.

Once the man had left them alone once again, Riley raised his wineglass and said, "To an evening filled with fun and laughter and good food."

Her fingers slid around her own glass and she touched the rim of it to his. "And to new friends, too. May they become good ones."

The sudden husky quality of her voice took him off guard. One moment she'd been piqued. The next she'd seemed inquisitive. And now? Well, now whatever it was that hummed in the air was steamy enough to wilt the romaine on their plates.

Her gaze seemed to darken even as he stared. "Of course," he murmured. "To new friends."

Without breaking eye contact, they drank deeply.

An hour and a half later, they were back in the car.

"Dinner was lovely," Catherine said.

"I worked at the restaurant for a while as a kid. I bused tables, washed dishes, anything they needed me to do." The owners had taken a gamble on him, and in doing so had given him a second chance. He'd spend the rest of his life feeling grateful. But he preferred that Catherine—and everyone else he'd ever meet—never know the details of that part of his life. In fact, he planned to do all he could to keep his secrets to himself.

Before she could inquire further, he said, "Do you like music? Are you up for listening to a little jazz?"

"Oh, I love jazz."

Riley could feel excitement pulsing off her in waves.

"I'm having such a great time tonight, Riley. Thank you."

Her effusive appreciation made his chest swell. He was reaping far too much pleasure from making this woman happy.

The parking lot of Midnight Blues was nearly packed. Riley pulled his sports car into one of the few remaining spots at the very rear of the lot.

When they entered the club, the sultry strains of a clarinet weaved with a saxophone's smoky, soulful notes. A double bass was the glue that held the warm harmonics together.

Catherine tossed her evening bag down on an empty table and caught his hand in hers.

"Riley…"

The pleading in her tone and the scorching heat of her skin sliding softly against his hit him like a one, two sucker punch to the jaw.

"Can we dance?" She gave his fingers a tug, sending a message that she didn't intend to take no for an answer. "Please?"

The boldness she flaunted appalled Catherine. She'd been trained to be modest and reserved. If she were back at home, she'd have squelched the brashness that continued to nudge her and fill her with confidence she didn't normally have.

There was something about Riley. Something that liberated her. Something that made her feel not only limitless, but uninhibited, too. Her family would be shocked by her behavior, she was certain. But they were far away. Thank God!

Out on the dance floor, she twirled toward Riley, and his arms settled around her as if they'd been dancing partners a thousand times before. One of his strong hands clasped hers, and the other snuggled down low at the small of her back.

He smelled...

"Nice," she murmured, closing her eyes to enjoy him.

Like sandalwood and citrus.

Catherine splayed her palm against his chest and was surprised by how firm his pecs were beneath his dress shirt. Her heart pattered like a butterfly's wings. Flipping and fluttering.

"The music is nice," he said, thinking he was agreeing with her statement.

She only smiled up into his handsome face for a second before closing her eyes again.

They swayed and turned and rocked. The smooth tune seemed to fuse the two of them into one being, and they moved as a solitary unit.

Instinct had her pressing her temple to his cheek. "You're a good dancer," she whispered.

"So are you."

Each time he spoke, she felt the sexy vibration under the flat of her hand. Being pressed against him so tightly thrilled her more than anything else she'd ever experienced in her life.

Her insides were jittery and she decided the feeling was pure anticipation, the keen expectation of what the remainder of the night held in store. But she gently prodded the eagerness away. If she focused too much on what might happen later, she would miss the truly romantic moments taking place in the here and now.

Leaning back a fraction, she looked up into his face. Strong bone structure formed sharp angles she found more than just a little attractive. She zeroed in on his mouth.

She'd seen it formed into a firm slash that gave the impression he was displeased. And those lips all too often turned down into a frown. But at this moment, there was a softness there. A suppleness that had her wanting to explore.

How would his lips feel against hers?

Catherine's pulse quickened when she thought about the end of their evening. Would he kiss her good-night? That was the American tradition, wasn't it? For a man to kiss his date when he dropped her off at her door?

Royal protocol in Lextanya called for first dates to be chaperoned, and a chaste handshake was all any suitor was allowed. If the truth were to be known, Catherine had thanked the heavens for the strict etiquette many times over the years.

But tonight? Tonight she was grateful that no chaperone was watching her every move. Tonight she was hoping—praying—for a kiss.

But would it be soft? Warm and moist? Firm? Slow and languorous? Or furiously ardent? If she had her druthers, she'd prefer to experience his kiss in each of those forms. The thought had her grinning.

"What are you thinking?" he asked.

"Nothing. Nothing at all."

Nothing she could tell him, anyway.

The music faded, and when they started back to their table, she kept hold of his hand. This nervy conduct was so new to her. It made her tremble with excitement. It also made her feel empowered.

By the time the band had started another set, Riley had ordered them drinks. A glass of champagne for her, a club soda for him.

The bluesy tune and the bubbly wine relaxed Catherine, and she looked around the darkened room. Men and women danced close; other couples sat at the small, round tables, their heads huddled together intimately. Some people were there on their own, some of those obviously on the hunt, while others seemed happy to simply enjoy the band.

The place was perfect, so was the night. She felt so lucky to be in Portland, far away from her controlling father and her selfish sister. Far away from the awkward situation of meeting that awful, skirt-chasing—

No, she told herself. She would not think about Étienne. She would not think about what awaited her at home. She would enjoy tonight. The music, the champagne…and Riley.

Once she'd fully banished the bad thoughts, she sighed, feeling as if she were in heaven.

"Somebody pinch me," she said aloud.

Riley's invisible vibes drew her attention. A naughty twinkle flashed in his dark eyes.

"Be careful what you wish for," he teased.

Catherine's laugh was throaty.

Immediately, though, he checked himself. "I'm sorry," he murmured. "That was a little forward of me. I usually wait until the second date before I start blatantly flirting."

She knew he was teasing, and she cut her eyes coyly. "Don't you dare apologize, Riley Jacobs." On the very next breath, she said, "I wouldn't mind if you didn't wait to give me a pinch or two."

Had that tantalizing tone really come from her mouth?

Riley tossed back his head and laughed.

After downing the last remnants of her drink, she gave his arm a playful pull. "This music is calling to me. Dance with me." She stood, dragging him along with her.

It was after midnight when they left the club. That second glass of champagne had her feeling as light as air.

"We probably shouldn't have stayed out so late," she told Riley as he started the car's engine. "Do you have to be at the clinic early?"

As he backed out of the parking spot, he quipped, "One perk of being the acting director is that I don't have to punch a time clock." He stopped the car and smoothly changed gears. "I do have to be in a meeting by nine, though. But I'll be fine."

With her head in a haze, she leaned back against the soft leather seat, and before she realized it, they had arrived at her hotel.

The purring car silenced when Riley turned the key in the ignition.

Catherine opened her eyes and turned to look at him.

She parted her lips, and like a pack of deranged gymnasts, words began to somersault right out into the air.

"You are one good-looking man, Riley. Your eyes are so dark. But did anyone ever tell you that the chocolaty-brown color is flecked with amber? They're just so...nice." She frowned. "Nice is such a benign word, and not at all what I really want to say. But the right word just doesn't seem to be coming to me at the moment."

"That champagne has thickened your accent just a little. Not that I mind. I like the sound of it. A lot. How-ever—" his chocolate gaze lit with humor "—I think, Catherine, that you need to go to bed."

"Oh, Riley, I'd love to go to bed."

The corners of his sexy mouth tightened. "Alone. You need to go to bed alone."

Disappointment engulfed her like an unstoppable rising tide.

He pushed open his door and got out. As she watched his trek around the car, she had a vague feeling she should feel bad about what she'd said. But she certainly couldn't think why. She'd only told him the truth.

He opened her door. "Come on," he urged, helping her out of her seat. "Let's get you up to your room."

"Yes," she said. "Let's."

The moment she stepped out of the elevator and into the long corridor leading to her room, she was besieged with a flurry of impatient hope. She'd thought the ea-gerness she'd felt at the jazz club had been powerful. Being in Riley's arms, inhaling the woodsy scent of his cologne, she'd looked forward to his kiss. However, the expectation pulsing through her now actually made her knees weak.

Her hand trembled when she reached into her purse for her keycard. It took a moment to find it.

"Here," he said, plucking it deftly from her fumbling fingers, "allow me."

Before he could slide the plastic card into the electronic slot, she placed a quelling hand on his arm.

"But I don't want the evening to end yet. I'm having such a good time, Riley."

He was so close that she could feel the heat of him.

"Me, too, Catherine. And that's the honest truth. I'm only sorry I nearly ruined things over dinner by making light of the problems of the clinic's clients."

She shook her head. "Oh, no. Everyone's entitled to an opinion. I shouldn't have gotten so bent out of shape about it. It's just that…well, it's a sore subject with me, I guess."

"I understand that now."

"But what you said was interesting," she told him. "About the problem being in the perception. I can still hear my father's voice in my head calling me his Fat Cat. He used to tease me terribly. And I'm not so sure— No, I know there was nothing loving about it." She stopped long enough to moisten her lips. She frowned as a thought came to her. "You know, I always thought that my father didn't like me because I was fat. But it could have been that I was fat because my father didn't like me."

An odd sadness welled from somewhere deep inside her. As the thoughts entered her head, she let them trip off her tongue. "And to this very day, he doesn't like me. Do you suppose that he still sees me as that chubby child?"

She knew in her heart that she was making some very profound statements, asking some insightful questions. And they just might be pointing to life-altering realizations. But her thinking was fuzzy, and fatigue suddenly weighed her down.

Catherine blinked, and then looked up at Riley.

He'd gone very still beside her, studying her face intently.

"Would you like to come inside?" she asked.

"I don't think that's a good idea. It's late. And I do have to be at the clinic by nine."

She sighed, wondering what had happened to the magical feel of the evening. "It's just as well, I guess," she told him. "I really am ready for bed now." She knew there was not one iota of sexual implication in her voice.

He nodded silently and unlocked her door. Then, without stepping across the threshold, he leaned in and flipped on the light switch for her. His gallantry made her smile.

"You're a nice guy, Riley."

"Well," he began, "I guess it's time for me to say good night."

Catherine thought for certain that her bold energy had been totally depleted. But she surprised herself when she demanded, "You are going to kiss me, aren't you?"

Like flint against metal, her question sparked fresh heat into the yearning that had been flickering in her all evening long. Clearly, she'd kindled something in Riley, as well. His dark gaze became hooded and she could tell he was fighting a smile…and something else.

"Do you want me to kiss you?"

His tone had gone all gravelly, and a shiver coursed across Catherine's skin. A current seemed to crackle between them, and the air turned viscous and hot.

"I want that very much."

His eyes roved over her face, his expression so passionate that her breath caught and held. The pads of his fingers were featherlight against her jaw, and she got the impression that he feared touching her.

She let him tip up her chin, and, when he leaned toward her, she let her eyes flutter closed.

Ever so gently his mouth pressed to hers, his lips slightly parted. The moist heat of his tongue tasted her so quickly, she was left wondering if she'd completely imagined the magical moment. She thought she heard him drag in a breath.

The kiss had been short, yet it had also been so sweet that it made her heart—and other parts of her anatomy— ache with need.

"Good night, Catherine," he said softly.

He made to turn, but she reached out and stopped him. He'd left his dinner jacket in the car, had rolled up the cuffs of his shirt several turns. Dark curls lightly sprinkled his forearm; the muscles beneath the skin were lean and corded. She remembered how firm his chest had been when they'd danced. She gave his arm a little squeeze so that she'd have a memory to savor. Later on when she was in the dark…all alone.

"I'm going to work out at the clinic in the morning," she told him. "Then I'm attending a seminar. Will you be free for lunch? My treat."

His breathing seemed ragged and he looked rattled. Why she should feel elated by this was beyond her. Still, her joy soared.

"That would be great," he said.

And she smiled. "Until tomorrow, then."

He offered her a nod and then headed back toward the elevator.

Standing there with her rump holding open her door, Catherine mulled over the man. He had good taste in food and good taste in music. He could dance. And his kiss? Ah, his kiss was heavenly.

She only wished she had experienced a little more of it.

He had intriguing eyes, a gorgeous face. His body was fit, his chest, firm, his forearms, strong.

She watched him retreat down the hallway, and she tucked her bottom lip firmly between her teeth.

His butt wasn't so bad, either.

Four

At the age of forty-two, Carrie Martin knew she was much too young to be feeling this tired and washed out. She picked up her wineglass, took a sip and stared out the window into the darkness, suspecting that regret had a lot to do with her misery.

People usually described her as lively and vivacious. A private-school math teacher, Carrie was loved by most of her students. She had a knack with kids, a knack for teaching. She loved her little apartment back in San Francisco, loved living in California, and most of all she loved being close to her son, Jason, a student at UCLA.

Carrie should be on top of the world.

But she wasn't.

Her story was a long one, but tonight she was in the perfect mood to rummage around in the complexities of it. She slipped off her shoes and tucked her bare feet up on the couch.

It hadn't been that long since she'd realized that something was missing in her life. Something profound.

A name had been placed to that something back in the late spring. She'd been in San Francisco, a nasty cold having kept her home from work. Lying on the couch in her robe and fuzzy slippers, she'd been flipping the channels on the TV when the sight of her ex-husband shocked her to the point that the remote control had slipped right out of her fingers and hit the floor with a thump.

Richard Strokudnowski.

She'd given up her search for him nearly twenty years ago. Yet there he was, plain as day, on the television commercial, promoting his lifestyle and fitness seminars.

Yes, he'd grown older. The silver streaks in his hair were certainly proof of that. But who hadn't been changed by the passing years? She certainly had. Inside and out.

The man on the screen, she remembered, seemed to have mastered the art of the hard sell, almost to the point of being cloying. However, even back in college, Richard had possessed an unmatchable charm—he'd certainly charmed her right out of her panties very soon after they'd met—and that charisma was what had alerted Carrie that the man on the commercial really was her ex. Well, that magnetic personality had been one clue, and those warm brown eyes of his had been another.

As long as they'd been divorced, Carrie had never been able to forget the way Richard's dark eyes could make her flush with yearning.

It had taken her several moments to work it all out; he'd changed his name from Strokudnowski to Strong; he was advancing toward his goal of becoming famous; he'd become *the* veritable fitness guru in the Pacific Northwest.

Her whole life had changed as she'd stood there in front of her television, and it had gone through myriad twists and turns since, too—twists and turns that had finally landed her in Portland, Oregon.

At first, Carrie hadn't told anyone the news. Not her friends, and certainly not Jason. Her son didn't need the upset. At least, not until she could gather more information on the man who now called himself Dr. Richie.

And gather she had. She'd spent the next few weeks combing the Internet when she should have been grading papers. And the more facts she'd discovered about Dr. Richie, the angrier she'd become.

Somewhere on his trek up the celebrity ladder, Richard had tweaked and adjusted his past until his life had become a complete work of fiction. What nerve it had to take for someone to do such a thing!

There was no mention anywhere that he'd attended university in Florida. Or that he'd been married to his high school sweetheart. There was also no mention that he'd completely abandoned his wife and baby.

Now, now, a voice in the back of her head chided. Richard didn't know anything about Jason when he left. It isn't fair to hold that against him.

Yes, but it hadn't changed the fact that he'd left without a backward glance, or that he'd taken half the money they'd worked so hard to save. That thought had her taking another drink from her glass of merlot.

But he wouldn't have left had you not backed him into a corner about his dream. You tried to pressure him into settling down. You wanted him to abandon a perfectly viable goal, that of motivating people to better health. The fact that he intended to find fame and fortune doing just that should have been mere icing on the cake. He'd been so certain he could do it, even when the two of you had still been attending college.

Hot tears burned the backs of her eyelids as she whispered to the empty room, "But I was pregnant." That's why she'd pushed him to give up his dream and settle down.

God, but she'd felt so alone back then. Just as alone as she felt right now.

And what did your pushing accomplish? the voice taunted. A horrible argument that had boiled over to the size of the damned Everglades, is all. And it forced him to choose his dreams over you. Your pushing was what left you abandoned and alone.

A single tear blazed a hot trail down her face.

Richard had been the love of her life. And he hadn't been gone a week before she realized her mistake in letting him go. She'd regretted pressuring him. She'd regretted drawing that line-in-the-sand ultimatum.

She'd searched for him, but had come up high and dry. She'd been distraught.

Cradling her wineglass between both hands, Carrie sighed. The sound echoed out into the shadows of the stark, cramped, but utilitarian efficiency apartment.

Her life hadn't been completely dismal. She'd given birth to a gorgeous baby boy. Jason had been and continued to be the one bright light in her world. Eventually, she'd given up her search for Richard and settled into her role of single mom. Lord above, how she loved being a parent.

She'd filed for divorce, and had the papers sent to Richard's parents. The nasty couple had refused to tell her where Richard was, so she'd refused to tell them they were grandparents. The papers had been returned with Richard's signature less than a month later.

That was when she'd met and married Ralph Martin. He'd been just the kind of man she'd needed, both solid and dependable. He mightn't have been the most romantic of men, but he'd been a wonderful father for Jason. Carrie and Ralph had spent fifteen years together. He'd suffered with diabetes, and four years ago he'd died of complications associated with the disease, leaving her once again a single mom.

When Jason had moved across the country to attend UCLA, Carrie'd decided she needed a change of scenery. Being closer to her son wouldn't hurt, either. So she'd moved to San Francisco and found a job teaching mathematics in a small private school.

But knowing no one in the large west-coast city, Carrie had begun to ponder her past…and her ex. Soon her thoughts were overflowing with memories of Richard and the times they had spent together.

That was why seeing him on the TV had stunned her so. Her research on Dr. Richie had pointed to Portland, Oregon, and to the new Healthy Living Clinic he would be running. By the time summer vacation had rolled around, she'd made the decision to spend some time in Portland looking up the famous Dr. Richie.

Telling Jason of her plans had been difficult. She considered not telling him, but he'd taken on the role of protector since his stepfather had passed away, and he'd suspected there was more to her extended trip than a mere vacation.

So she'd gently broken the news to her son that she'd discovered the whereabouts of his biological father. She had told Jason the truth about Richard Strokudnowski when he'd been a boy, but they hadn't had reason to discuss him much over the years. She'd been honest about the fact that his father had never known he existed, and about the fact that she'd searched hard for Richard when Jason had been a baby.

She'd told her son before leaving San Francisco that she now regretted giving up her search all those years ago. And that she would never be content until she finally got the chance to see Richard and tell him that he had a son.

Jason had grown quiet, his feelings about Richard obviously mixed. However, he hadn't told his mother not to go.

So here she was in Oregon, having found a tiny apartment, a job as a hostess at La Grenouille Dorée, one of Portland's fanciest restaurants. She'd been visiting the Healthy Living Clinic and had even attended some of Richard's seminars.

When she'd first seen him up there on that stage, his personality had appeared to be too slick, almost shifty, and she hadn't been sure she wanted to reveal herself to him at all. But she sensed pain in the depths of his dark eyes. Pain...and what she took as loneliness.

Her weeks in Portland had been roller-coaster-crazy on her emotions. She'd ping-ponged between feeling sympathetic toward the man she'd once been married to, and wanting to rip his handsome face off for so thoroughly forgetting her, wiping her right out of his past.

And it was during one of these terrible moments of raging resentment that she'd stood up and lambasted him right in the middle of one of his workshops.

She couldn't have embarrassed either of them more had she painstakingly planned it.

He'd stormed out of the room, out of the clinic and gone into hiding. That had been over a week ago.

Because of her, he was in a frightful mess and his job at the clinic was on the line. The new director... What was his name? Dr. Riley Jacobs, she remembered. He'd been nice enough with his promise of finding Richard so he could help with the planned testing of NoWait.

Suddenly, though, doubt set in. What if Dr. Jacobs's story was all a lie and the clinic wanted to lure Richard in there to publicly fire him? All because she'd—

Hold on! The voice that had chided her only a moment before was now softer and more consoling. This fix Richard is in is his own doing. He's the one who'd rewritten his past for those who hired him. He's the one who came up with the crazy idea of that NoWait oil.

"Homeopathic therapy, my butt," Carrie muttered. Why, Richard couldn't mix his way out of a child's chemistry set, let alone come up with a topical weight-loss treatment that would actually work.

Users of NoWait had become perceptibly passionate, and there was no way to hide the fact that it was that damned oil that was causing it. The NoWait zealots didn't seem to care that kissing complete strangers simply wasn't done. Why, she'd even read one newspaper article about a married couple she'd seen buying NoWait at the clinic. The man and his wife had become so overcome with their desire for each other that they had done the dirty deed in broad daylight—in a public park, no less. They'd been arrested, of course, but so far neither the authorities nor the reporter who had written the article had put all the pieces together.

But it was only a matter of time before the truth would be exposed.

The people running the clinic knew. That was why they were attempting to confiscate all the NoWait. That's why they wanted to find Richard, too. She hoped and prayed that Dr. Jacobs had been telling her the truth about wanting Richard to help in the lab with the tests.

Yes, Richard, with his rash schemes to become famous, had been his own worst enemy.

Carrie set the glass on the end table, her fingers trembling. Then she snapped on the light. Sitting in the dark was only contributing to her bad mood.

There was no way around feeling guilty for the way she'd acted. For the awful accusations she'd flung at Richard right in front of his colleagues and all those despairing people who needed his help losing weight.

Carrie desperately wanted to find Richard. To tell him she was sorry. To tell him the clinic wanted him. Needed him.

To tell him about his son.

Richard Strong was the profound "something" her life had been missing for so long. That much was a certainty. However, there were so many unanswered questions rolling around in her mind. She needed to know if he ever thought about her. If he had ever missed her over the years. If he, like she, had wished that things could have turned out differently for them.

She needed to know if he could forgive her.

She would never be happy until she had some answers. But answers weren't possible until she found Richard.

Where on earth could he be?

The following morning Riley sat at the conference table with Faye Lassen, a slew of Portland General's administrators, various laboratory personnel and several others whose names, titles and interest in the NoWait testing he was oblivious to. He'd been sitting in this meeting for well over two hours, but everyone might as well have been speaking a foreign language for as much as he'd gotten out of it.

Catherine consumed his thoughts. Every time he attempted to concentrate on the topic at hand, something about her would whisper across his brain. Something she'd said, or something she'd done, or some expression on her angelic face.

She'd had him running the full emotional gamut last night.

Her shamelessness had stunned him. Yet each time she'd made some bold move, it was immediately followed up by a flash of uncertainty that he'd suspected she'd been unaware of. But Riley had seen it, time and again, and he had thought it was so sweet. It had been patent proof to him that her overly confident behavior probably wasn't the norm for her.

She'd made him laugh, and she hadn't minded looking silly to do it. At one point she'd cracked a self-deprecating joke that had him laughing so hard his cheek muscles had begun to ache.

The complexity of her moods had intrigued him.

She'd annoyed the hell out of him at the restaurant when they'd talked about whether or not the clinic's clients suffered with real problems. He'd tried to make her understand his position, and that he hadn't meant to make light of their situations, but he simply couldn't compare the medical needs of someone needing to lose a couple of pounds with someone in the throes of a life-threatening illness. However, she'd stubbornly stood by her opinion that the people in the clinic deserved just as much attention as anyone else. He'd let it drop, silently deciding they should agree to disagree.

At the end of the evening, however, she'd made him understand a little better about the sufferings of overweight people. When she'd spoken about her treatment at the hands of her father—his callous name-calling, his withholding of affection—the vulnerability that emanated from her had disturbed him greatly. All he'd wanted to do was wrap his arms around her, hold her tight and make all the pain go away.

Catherine had scars from her past. And from the way she talked about her relationship with her father, she might very well be acquiring more scars even as an adult who had conquered her childhood weight problem.

Catherine had stirred his desire. When he'd first picked her up, her physical appearance had blown him away. And later, with her body pressed up tight against his at Midnight Blues, Riley's insides had writhed with wild, primal urges. He wanted her, there could be no doubt about that.

And then she'd bluntly insisted that he kiss her goodnight… He grinned even now, thinking about it. He'd been so plagued with need that he feared he would lose all control. But he hadn't, and the only reason had been because she'd just finished looking so damned defenseless when she'd talked about her past. He'd been determined not to take advantage of her in that state. So when he'd kissed her, he'd been shooting for physical contact that would measure in the platonic range. But even the small, swift peck he'd given her had missed that mark. He'd spent the remainder of last night tossing and turning while his subconscious continued to conjure sensuous images of how easily that chaste kiss could have turned outrageously erotic, and once he'd finally dropped off to sleep, it had done just that in his dreams.

His whole body grew hot as he contemplated the sub-liminal night fantasy.

"Riley?"

Dr. David Graham was older than Mount Hood, and the man should have retired years ago. But his position as director and top dog—as he'd preferred to refer to himself—at Portland General Hospital had afforded him a great deal of clout and power, and a sort of celebrity in the city that he refused to give up. Everyone knew Dr. Graham would have to be carried from his prestigious office feet first.

"Yes?" Riley sat up straighter in his chair.

"I was asking your thoughts on the matter," David said, obviously unhappy that he'd had to backtrack to bring Riley up to par. "You haven't said much at all."

Riley had no idea exactly which matter he meant. Dr. Graham had been the one who'd forced Riley into this job, with promises of great things to come for him if he saved the clinic from ruin once the truth about Dr. Richie had been made public. However, the offer had also held overtones that smacked of blackmail, and Riley hated the fact that his past could be used against him.

"One of the concerns Dr. Jacobs and I talked about," Faye Lassen supplied for him, "is the price tag of the project. It might be cost-effective for us to contract an outside laboratory for the testing."

Riley cast her a grateful glance, but she seemed too focused on the goings-on of the meeting to notice.

David Graham looked appalled by Faye's suggestion. "And risk allowing this information to get out?"

Faye didn't wither under the director's frown. "You know contract labs are run under strict proprietary information laws, Dr. Graham. Everything about our experiments, from the substance to the results, will be safe."

David's wiry brows set stubbornly. "I want to keep this in-house. And I've already agreed that Dr. Richie should head this up. Dr. Jacobs was right when he told me last week that NoWait is Richard Strong's baby. No one knows the stuff like he does." Frustration evidently got the better of him and he thumped his hand on the table. "Why can't we find that man?"

A dropped pin would have clashed like a cymbal in the sudden silence.

The bristly director frowned down at the long agenda in front of him. "We still have a lot to discuss, and I see it's nearly lunchtime. But I think it's imperative that we nail everything down today. I don't want this to drag on with endless meetings. I want the testing started. Or at the very least, I want all of our ducks in a row so that when Dr. Richie returns he can get right on it.

"We'll order lunch in," he announced. "Faye, can you take care of it?"

Automatically, Faye answered, "Certainly, Dr. Graham."

"Have the food delivered right here." To the group at large he said, "Let's take a twenty-minute break. That should give all of you time to reschedule your afternoon appointments, and then we can get right back on this, okay?"

He might have formed the words into a question, but he wasn't interested in anyone's opinion. He clearly expected his wants to be fully met.

Riley and Faye left the meeting together. Once they were out of hearing range, Riley said, "Thanks for that back there."

Faye smiled. "No problem. You'd do it for me if the situation had been reversed."

He nodded.

"By the way," she quipped, "where were you? Or rather, where were your thoughts? You were positively lost."

He wasn't sure how to answer the question. He'd taken Catherine out last night, shown her a bit of Portland. Their evening together had even been referred to as a date. But it wasn't as if this…thing between them was going anywhere.

Faye shoved her heavy glasses up on her nose. "Ah, so it's a woman."

Female intuition never ceased to amaze him.

They turned a corner in the maze of the hospital and headed for the main lobby. "It's nothing," he muttered. She shot him a dubious look, and he asserted, "Really."

They walked in silence for several seconds.

Faye said, "What do you think about the way Dr. Graham is pushing to get this testing started?"

"I don't like it. If it's rushed, mistakes are bound to be made."

The expression on her face told him she agreed.

"If we're going to do the testing here," he continued, "we should get our best toxicologists on it. We should leave this to the experts. And Dr. Richie really should be involved even if it's only as a consultant."

She nodded.

Sunlight streamed though the glass-enclosed lobby. Faye's steps slowed.

"I have to run downstairs to the cafeteria to order sandwiches."

Riley gritted his teeth. "That shouldn't be your job."

Faye waved away his concern. "I don't mind. And someone's got to do it."

He caught and held her gaze. "Someday," he said, "you're going to get full credit for all you do."

Her cheeks tinged pink with embarrassment, and Riley silently surmised that she'd be a very attractive woman if she'd loosen those tight fasteners from her hair and unmask herself from those enormous eyeglasses.

But he quickly curbed the thought. Faye Lassen was an excellent doctor and an inordinately organized and efficient administrator. That in itself should be enough.

He offered, "Do you want me to get the receptionists started on rearranging your afternoon appointments?"

"No, thanks. I'll call them on my cell on my way to the cafeteria."

"Okay, then, I'll see you back in the meeting in twenty."

They separated, and then Riley turned back and called out to her. "Do you have any idea which session Catherine Houston was going to attend this morning? I was supposed to have lunch with her today, so I need to cancel."

Faye's face brightened. "Is Catherine the woman who had you so engrossed all morning?"

His mouth drew into a line of warning.

"Okay, okay," she said, chuckling. "It's none of my business. It's just that she and I have become kind of chatty. She's a sweet person, Riley. We're going out this weekend, as a matter of fact. She asked me to show her the best shops.

"Anyway," Faye continued, "Catherine told me she was looking for a fun workshop. So she chose that popular one on self-control. Um…" Faye thought a second. "Oh, yes. Mind over Manicotti, it's called. I'm sure that's where you'll find her."

"Thanks."

Riley walked out into the sunshine, hardly aware of the glorious day.

So Catherine had chosen to attend a session on self-control, he thought. Funny, last night at the restaurant she'd chosen a simple salad and a meatless pasta sauce. She hardly seemed to have a lack of self-control. Well, where food had been concerned, she hadn't. However, if flirtation were chocolate syrup, she'd have drowned in the rich confection last night. Her verbal play had been enticing, to say the least.

She'd made him feel some powerful physical urges. She'd stirred a hunger in him. A hunger so deep it had been awesome to experience, and nearly impossible to quell. If he hadn't witnessed those extremely vulnerable moments—the raw pain that had cast shadows in her blue eyes when she'd talked about her father and her lonely childhood—he might have unleashed his craving for her. He just might have satiated his need.

When he'd noticed that the champagne had made her tipsy, he'd suggested she should sleep it off.

I'd love *to go to bed.*

Her unashamedly sexual response had blown him away. The mere thought of her innuendo made heat coil down deep in his core even now. Sweat prickled his brow and he gulped in a lungful of fresh, mind-clearing air. Only then did an errant thought sough through his head.

Upper crust. Faye had clued him in even before he'd met Catherine. And Catherine had cemented the idea herself last night at the gardens.

Perfume from France, indeed. Made just for her. Riley shook his head as he pulled open the front door of the clinic.

Catherine Houston was a blue blood.

Her name alone made his thinking go hazy. She was a blue blood who smelled like sun-warmed jasmine…who had creamy skin, golden hair and high, rounded—

Riley gave himself a mental shake. He'd had his share

of humiliation from the likes of the well-to-do to last him a lifetime and beyond.

Like a coiled snake, the vile memory hissed and bared its teeth at him. He'd vowed that he'd never put himself in a situation where it might be repeated.

Maybe canceling lunch was a good thing. Staying away from Catherine would be for the best.

After checking with reception to find out which conference room was being used for the Mind over Manicotti workshop, Riley stalked down the hall and let himself into the room as quietly as possible. He stood in the back to let his eyes adjust to the soft lights.

The speaker at the podium was a jovial woman whose humorous personal insights never failed to make the workshop attendees relax and enjoy themselves in the lighthearted session.

Riley spotted Catherine in the crowd immediately. He hadn't been lying last night when he'd told her there was nothing ordinary about her. Her long, wavy hair glowed flaxen even in the low lighting.

Luckily, there was an empty seat right next to her. He headed down the aisle.

"Catherine," he whispered as he sat.

The smile she offered him lightened his heart. Hell, it brightened his whole damned day!

Down, boy! he ordered his thoughts. And other parts of his libido.

"Hi," she whispered back, her sweet, sexy accent flowing over him like warm honey.

Riley firmed his jaw. "I have to cancel lunch," he said. "I'll be stuck in a meeting all afternoon."

He should probably apologize. However, he didn't make a habit of dishonesty merely for politeness' sake.

Her beautiful face went blank. Although she struggled to hide her emotions, he couldn't miss her disappointment.

Guilt poked at him like a sharp stick, but he refused to allow it to force him to say something he didn't mean. Missing this lunch date was a good thing; he had to keep repeating that to himself.

When it looked as though disillusionment had begun to win in her battle of wills, Riley couldn't take it any longer. "I just wanted to let you know," he whispered. Without allowing himself to think further, he pushed himself up from the chair and headed toward the door at the back of the conference room.

Five

The Pearl District was an area of the city filled with block after block of bistros, boutiques, numerous galleries, two art schools, salons, florists and a host of other shops. It was a place where old met new. Where abandoned manufacturing plants had been transformed into wine shops, bakeries and much-sought-after loft apartments. And Catherine was thoroughly charmed by it all.

"This place used to be nothing but old warehouses and weedy, littered lots," Faye told Catherine.

The two of them bustled down the street as only women on a shopping mission could, various bags swinging on their arms.

Faye continued, "And who would ever believe that people would want to live overlooking the rail yard? But Old Union Station now has a great restaurant and a piano bar. The Pearl is a thriving community."

"The city's done a great job renovating the area, that's for sure." Catherine looked for traffic and then stepped out into the street.

"Careful of those," Faye warned, pointing to the new streetcar tracks embedded in the roadway. "Don't get your heel caught."

The boutique they entered had some lovely clothing on display.

Faye scanned one particular dress from top to bottom, but rather than give her opinion of the fabric or the style of the dress, she casually asked, "So what's happening between you and Riley?"

The urge to roll her eyes in response was nearly overwhelming, but Catherine's years of deportment training forced her to overcome it. "Not a thing, it seems. I got him to take me out. Once. And we had a great time. Or so I thought." Lifting the hem of the dress on display, she studied the workmanship. "Underneath that grumpiness I found a nice guy."

She remembered the excruciatingly sweet kiss they'd shared. Murmuring, she wickedly corrected, "A yummy guy, actually."

Faye laughed.

Catherine let the fabric fall from her fingers. "But then he canceled our lunch date the next day. And I suspect he's been avoiding me ever since."

Faye chose a dress from the rack. "I think I'll try this on."

Catherine shook her head. "Not that one." She took the dress and hung it back on the rack. "Everything you wear is tan or cream or brown. You need some color, Faye." She picked a shirtdress in a rich shade of burnt orange, just perfect for September.

"I can't," Faye exclaimed.

"Of course, you can. It'll look great."

Faye dug in her heels, and Catherine laughed, giving her a little shove. "The least you can do is try it on." She snatched up a few more colorful items in the same size. "And it won't hurt to try these, too."

They laughed like school chums all the way back to the dressing room.

From behind the curtain, Faye continued with the important part of their ongoing conversation, "If it's any consolation, Riley really was stuck in an all-day meeting. I was stuck there with him."

Catherine held a fuzzy pink top in place under her chin and looked at her reflection while waiting for her friend. "That doesn't explain why he's been sidestepping me at every turn. Makes a girl feel unwanted."

Faye stepped out of the cubical, and Catherine gasped.

"It's perfect," she told Faye, excitement energizing her tone. "That color makes your eyes just pop."

"I don't know—"

"Don't be ridiculous! It's perfect." Catherine edged around until she was between Faye and the mirror. She hoped she wasn't being too intrusive, but she asked, "Faye, would you take your hair down? I'd like to see how long it is."

The woman's blue eyes darted toward the floor.

"Oh, don't go all shy on me now." Catherine plunked a playful fist on her hip. "I've bared my soul about Riley and how he's made me feel. All I've asked you to do is try on a few clothes and take the pins from your hair."

"Okay, okay." Faye removed the clip securing her twist and shook her head, releasing her brown tresses.

"Wow! It's so shiny." Boldly, Catherine reached up and

slid Faye's glasses off her face. "Have you ever thought about contacts? These glasses hide your lovely eyes."

Faye flinched, but she allowed her eyeglasses to be removed.

Catherine blinked. "Faye, you're beautiful."

"No, I'm not."

"Oh, but you are." Catherine circled her friend. "And the cut of that dress!" She let out a low whistle. "Really accentuates the back stairwell, if you know what I mean. I vote that you buy it."

"I can't buy this," Faye said. "It would be a waste of money. I don't wear clothes like this to work." Her mouth twisted ironically. "And I barely have time to go home and feed my cat, let alone find time for a life outside the clinic."

That stopped Catherine in her tracks. "But why?" Faye was only six years older than she; surely she had a whole life in front of her.

Uneasiness had Faye's body tensing. Catherine knew immediately that she'd probed into something much too personal.

She was about to apologize and back her way out of the subject when Faye softly said, "It's my own fault."

A perceptible heaviness had the air in the small dressing-room area feeling thick. Catherine waited to see if Faye intended to tell her more.

"I've been working on getting the health clinic off the ground for years," she told Catherine. "People don't realize how much planning goes into such a business endeavor."

"You helped with the inception of the idea?" Bewilderment knit Catherine's brow. "But I read the newspaper accounts. Your name wasn't mentioned once. It was, um—" she tapped her chin, trying to remember "—a Dr. David—"

"Graham." A storm churned in Faye's blue eyes. "Yeah, once the clinic received approval and the plans were drawn up, he sort of took over as spokesperson. Whenever the public was involved, anyway. But I was the one in the trenches."

"How unfair."

Faye shrugged. "All that mattered to me was to see my idea come to fruition. Anyway, back to why I don't have a life. Early on, I hawked my proposal to anyone who would listen. First, I had to convince the hospital administrators and the Board of Directors. And once they'd approved the idea, I had to meet with city officials and persuade them that the clinic would be a good thing for Portland.

"And after everyone gave the go ahead," she continued, "I was up to my neck in meetings with architects and engineers, building permit people and Board of Variance committee members, contractors and building inspectors."

She sighed, her shoulders rounding. "I became like a madwoman intent on seeing my vision fulfilled." Faye paused, moistened her lips, concentrated on her reflection in the mirror as she softly revealed, "It cost me my marriage."

"Oh, honey." Catherine placed a comforting hand on her friend's arm. "I'm sorry."

Faye's spine straightened and her chin tipped up courageously. "It was my own fault. I didn't give my husband the time he needed. The time he deserved. By the time I realized my mistake, it was too late."

Giving her arm a squeeze, Catherine murmured, "I'm sorry about the divorce."

"I'm not divorced. Yet. We're separated. But I get sick to my stomach every day when I collect the mail, sure that the papers are going to arrive."

There was no proper response she could think of to make, so Catherine simply remained silent.

Absently, Faye smoothed the cuff of the shirtdress. "Anyway, Mark had left, so I bent my head into the wind and kept working on getting the clinic built. It was difficult. Since the construction industry is a male-dominated world, I made myself as professional as possible." She turned to face Catherine. "The result is the no-frills, no-fun, take-no-guff woman standing before you." She attempted to smile, but the result was kind of sad.

Catherine's thoughts started whirling as she tried to think of a positive spin to place on all that Faye had said. Finally, she blurted, "So it's all a mask. The real you is hiding in there somewhere."

Quietly, but firmly, Faye said, "And that's exactly how I want to keep it."

Confusion knitted Catherine's brow. "But why, Faye? You're a beautiful—"

"I'm not," Faye insisted, cutting Catherine off. "I don't like the real me, to tell you the truth. The real me got her priorities all screwed up. She messed up everything and now she just has to live with what she's done."

Empathy made Catherine's heart go all warm and fuzzy. "You're being way too hard on yourself. The clinic is a wonderful place. And you were the one who made it happen." She shifted, her head tilting a fraction. "Faye, since the clinic was your baby, why aren't you running the place?"

"Oh, that was David Graham's idea," she said. "He felt we needed someone flashy in the job. That's why he had me recruit Dr. Richie. And I was made second in command."

Catherine could tell the subject was a bone sliver that stuck in Faye's craw.

"But now he's gone," Catherine couldn't help but point out, "and Riley's in the position. Does Dr. Graham even know you're interested in the job?"

"I'm a woman, Catherine. Dr. Graham hasn't promoted a woman to a top managerial position in, well, ever." Faye raised an agitated hand to her hair, fidgeting. "It doesn't really matter. All that matters is that the clinic is open to the public."

Catherine opened her mouth to respond, but Faye exclaimed, "What am I saying? Of course, it matters. Running the clinic should have been my job."

Meeting Catherine's gaze in the mirror, Faye's eyes went wide. "I'm sorry. That was a terrible outburst."

"Don't apologize. I'm just happy you feel safe enough to confide in me."

"I like Riley," Faye rushed to say. "And he's doing a great job at the clinic. It was actually good of him to accept it since things are such a shambles."

"Yes. But he's not really happy there."

Evidently, Faye hadn't noticed. "Really? Wow, what I wouldn't give to become director." She heaved a frustrated sigh. "But Dr. Graham won't go for it."

"Surely he knows of all you've done up to this point."

"I'm not sure he does. Although I have no idea why he wouldn't. He's got this way of overlooking me."

"Well, we've got to change that," Catherine announced. "And wearing this dress to work on Monday—with your hair down—is just the start!"

"I don't know that I want to be noticed for my physical

attributes, Catherine." Faye attempted to take a backward step. "I want to be respected for my brains and my ability."

"As you said, you're a woman. And as a woman you have to use your brains and your ability and whatever attributes you can to get ahead."

"But—"

"No buts. Get in there and try on those other outfits."

For several long seconds, Catherine feared her friend would refuse. But suddenly Faye's beautiful eyes lit with excitement, and something else, too. Determination? And with a new purpose, she spun on her toe and disappeared into the cubicle.

Not too much later they were back out on the sidewalk with several new shopping bags in tow.

"Thanks, Catherine," Faye said, her cheeks flushed with marvelous color. "That was so much fun."

"The fun isn't over. We passed a salon." She indicated up the street with a jerk of her head. "Let's go have a facial—my treat. And then I want to show you how a little makeup can set off your best features."

Faye admitted, "I've never been big on makeup. Never really had the time."

"If you want to be noticed—and you deserve to be, Faye—then you'll start taking the time. Besides, you don't need a lot," Catherine assured her. "It's all in the technique. And believe me when I tell you that there was a time when technique was all I had going for me."

"Oh, stop." Faye smiled, and when Catherine didn't return it, she looked askance. "You are kidding, right?"

Catherine shook her head. "I was a real ugly duckling all through my teens. But I like to think I've conquered most of my problems."

"But…I don't understand. You're gorgeous."

Laughter was Catherine's best defense against her dark past. "Yeah, well, I'm obviously not gorgeous enough for some people."

Luckily, Faye was astute enough to pick up the particular person to whom Catherine was alluding.

"Listen, I shouldn't say too much. Riley is my boss and all that." Faye's voice lowered as she said, "But I think we should talk about…you know…what you can do."

"I wish I knew what to do. I can't even seem to capture his attention. Mmm, maybe if I walked into the clinic stark naked…?"

Faye laughed. "No, please. We don't want the police involved. But what I was thinking was a lure of some kind."

Intrigued, Catherine slowed her steps, not wanting to miss a single word.

"I know that Riley's a sports buff," Faye continued. "I see him reading the sports pages. He particularly likes basketball, but the Trail Blazers don't start playing until the end of October." Faye paused, then said, "How about tickets to an air show? There's one going on just outside Portland this weekend. Airplanes are big and loud. And these do fancy spins and loops and other death-defying stunts."

"I agree that would be very much a man-thing."

"And they sell hot dogs, too."

"Hot dogs? You mean like sausages?"

"Sort of. They're a foot long, served on warm toasted buns and smothered in mustard."

"And American men like these foot-long hot dogs?"

"They love them!"

"So, trick planes and hot dogs? Why, you wicked woman." Catherine chuckled. "I think I love you! How and where do I get tickets?"

A smile flashed across Faye's face. "We can ride out to Hillsboro Airport this afternoon and pick up tickets for to-morrow's show."

"Okay, but I still have a bit of a problem. If I buy tick-ets for tomorrow, how do I reach Riley to invite him? He's gotten awfully good at evading me. "

"I know the man's schedule like the back of my hand," Faye bragged. "And he's fairly consistent. He doesn't ac-tually work Saturdays and Sundays, but he always shows his face at the clinic, walks around greeting everyone, checking things out. I know exactly where he'll be tomor-row morning at nine. If we coordinate this right, he'll be trapped." Her eyes glittered as only a cunning woman's could. "He'll be ours." Murmuring, she quickly corrected, "Or rather, yours."

A bold and daring thrill shot through Catherine clean to the tips of her toes. "Air-show tickets, foot-long hot dogs and a fiendish plan of attack. I'd say Riley is one man who is pretty much done for, wouldn't you?"

Catherine stood at the end of the long corridor, her heart in her throat. What if, she wondered, Riley turned her down after she'd gone to all this trouble?

All this trouble?

The only trouble she'd gone to was to conspire with Faye in order to be alone with Riley. Scheming and conniving were so out of the realm of normal for a von Husden. Cather-ine knew her father would be appalled. She also knew she should feel wretched about cornering Riley like this.

As she waited for Faye's signal, Catherine was plagued with many emotions. She grinned. Excitement, yes. Exhilaration, yes. Mischievousness, oh yes! But shame? Not even a smidgen.

Well, maybe a smidgen, but it wasn't enough to keep her from going through with her plan.

When Catherine saw Riley enter the clinic, she took a quick moment to ogle those broad shoulders of his and then she ducked back behind the corner so he wouldn't see her. She had no idea what it was about Riley that had her feeling this overwhelming…something.

She couldn't even put a name to what he made her feel. All she knew was the urge to see him, to be with him, was great. She felt like a schoolgirl in pursuit of her first beau.

But you aren't a schoolgirl, the voice in her head warned. You're an adult. A grown woman.

"All the better," she whispered gleefully. The tactics employed by a mature woman could be oh-so-much-more seductive. Catherine had to slap her hand across her mouth to keep from snickering out loud.

True to her word, Faye fell into step with Riley when he was about halfway down the hall. Catherine listened as they greeted each other and then chatted about various issues pertaining to clinic business. They stopped, as Faye had predicted, right in front of the door that led to the staff break room, not two feet from where Catherine was hiding.

"So everything's running smoothly," Faye said.

"Thanks for the update. But what are you doing here on a Sunday?" he asked.

Catherine tensed, but Faye's tone was completely relaxed as she replied, "Oh, I didn't have any plans and I thought I'd just check in. How about you? Do you have any plans today?"

What a nervy woman that Faye was, Catherine silently surmised. If the von Husdens ever wanted to usurp a country some day in the future, Catherine wouldn't hesitate to recruit Faye as a spy.

"Nah," Riley said. "I'm just going to get a cup of coffee and then head to my office. There's a stack of journals waiting to be read."

"Sounds exciting." There was a smile in Faye's voice. "Well, I'll see you around, then."

"Faye—" Riley paused, then Catherine heard the leather soles of his shoes scuff as he shifted his weight. "Did you change your hair? It looks nice."

Elation welled in Catherine. Riley was sweet to notice that Faye was wearing her hair down today. It would boost Faye's ego, Catherine knew.

"Thanks, Riley." Pleasure brightened Faye's words, and then Catherine heard her friend's footsteps retreating down the corridor.

The handle of the break-room door clicked and the hinges gave a slight squeak. Then Catherine heard the door close, presumably behind Riley.

He was in the break room. All alone.

Trapped.

With her heart thudding a powerful beat, Catherine stole from her hiding place and stood in front of the break-room door. Faye turned around, gave her a smile and a thumbs-up sign for luck. After returning the signal and adding a hasty wave of thanks, Catherine inhaled deeply and focused all her energy into launching her attack.

Riley's dark gaze widened when she entered the room.

"Catherine."

Surprise, surprise!

A smile trailed over her lips. She couldn't have stopped it had she wanted to, which she didn't. For some reason, she didn't care if he spoke her name with surprise or happiness or irritation. All she knew was that she liked the way her name rumbled from his throat.

"Hi, there," she greeted softly, silkily. "I know it's only been a few days, but I feel like it's been ages since I've seen you."

"Yeah." He looked nervous as he poured coffee into his mug. "I've been busy with meetings and…well, more meetings. Coffee?"

"I'd love some." She sauntered across the tiny room, pulled a foam cup from the stack and held it out toward him. Rich steam wafted and Catherine made a big deal of inhaling it, closing her eyes, expanding her chest and playing up her breasts to their best advantage by arching her spine just the slightest bit. She guessed that was how a woman would use her wiles to capture a man's attention.

"Smells good," she murmured.

She glanced up at him through lowered lashes, pleased to see that his gaze had zeroed right in on the pair of bull's eyes she'd presented just for him. She'd worn a fine-gauge sweater in palest pink, and her trousers fit her rather snugly. She'd chosen the outfit to show off all that she had to offer him. Clearly, he'd noticed.

"Thank you," she said.

"Welcome."

Although he hadn't actually added anything to his cup, he stirred the liquid almost vigorously. Catherine wanted to chuckle at his agitation, but she didn't.

"I've missed you."

"Yeah, well…" he began to say as he backed up a half step, "I've been busy—"

"With meetings," she finished for him. She moved forward a half step, luxuriating in the enjoyment of just being close to him, even if it might end up being only for a moment or two. "You know, sometimes you have to make time for your friends. We are friends, aren't we, Riley?"

"Of course, Catherine."

"I mean, I didn't do anything the night we went out that upset you, did I?" She splayed her free hand on his chest and felt the heat of him penetrating his shirt.

"Of course not, Catherine."

"Good," she said. "Then there's no reason why you shouldn't accept my invitation to the air show. It's going on all day out at Hillsboro Airport. I've got tickets. It'll be fun."

His handsome face blanched. He truly looked like a snared rabbit.

Fearing that his refusal might totally crush her spirit, Catherine decided to inject some humor into the moment.

Pursing her lips, she displayed the sexiest pout she could muster. Then she begged, "Please say you'll go, Riley." She blinked a couple of times for good measure. "I just don't know how much longer I can keep up this sex-pot routine. It's an awful lot of work."

In an instant, all fear left Riley's face and he laughed.

The appealing sound had her making one final attempt at playing the seductress. "Come on, Riley. I want you to go with me. It'll be fun. Besides, I've never had an American sausage. I'd love one smothered in mustard."

His laughter died a quick death, but his gaze continued to blaze with nefarious humor.

It became obvious quickly that he was putting great effort into remaining straight-faced, attempting not to laugh at what she'd said. When she realized her faux pas, heat rushed to her face and she backed up a step.

"Some sexy siren I make," she muttered, all traces of the Mistress of Enchantment gone. "I didn't mean that the way it came out. Really I didn't. I meant a hot dog, Riley. I want an American hot dog."

His brown eyes were actually tearing now, and his shoulders were quaking.

"That didn't sound much better, did it?"

"No," he admitted, "it didn't. But I don't mind telling you that I'd fight off a whole army of men if they tried to get between me and a bottle of mustard."

Catherine laughed, and Riley joined her.

Before either of them had taken a single sip of their coffee, he agreed to spend the day with her. On their way out of the clinic, Catherine caught Faye's eye and offered her a wink of victory.

Hillsboro was a small, nine-hundred-acre landing field, but even though it only boasted two runways, the air show's master of ceremonies was happy to inform the crowd, it was the second busiest airport in the state of Oregon.

An antique biplane puttered in the clear sky overhead, and when it dipped low to the ground, the wing-walking passenger wowed everyone present, including Catherine.

She told Riley, "I wouldn't have the nerve to do that."

"I wouldn't have the balance."

As silly as it seemed, Riley made the sunshine brighter. He made the day more exciting.

Or maybe it was simply that being with him made her so amazingly happy.

Next, they watched a pair of professional pilots who called themselves the Masters of Disaster. They flew their planes in what looked to be a wild and out-of-control dogfight, complete with billowing trails of thick smoke and shooting flames. Their death-defying maneuvers had the crowd on edge. Tension rippled across the throng like an electric current.

One pilot performed a nosedive that made Catherine so nervous she latched on to Riley's arm without even realizing it.

At what seemed the very last possible second, the plane pulled out of the dive and soared back up into the blue, cloudless sky. Then another plane swooped so close to the first that Catherine gasped, clutching Riley tighter.

"It's like a tightly choreographed dance," he said softly, his gaze tipped upward.

"Doesn't look like any dance I've ever seen."

The MC announced that a pair of United States Air Force F-16s would be paying a visit. He'd no sooner made the broadcast than Catherine's entire body flinched at the deafening sound of the jets overhead. They were an awesome sight to behold.

"Oh, my," she breathed. "We don't have anything like that where I come from."

"And where do you come from?"

Anxiety flashed through her, and she didn't respond immediately. She was extremely reluctant to tell him about Lextanya, fearing she would blow her cover. Finally, she said, "I'm from a small European country. An island in the Mediterranean." She clamped her lips shut.

At first, she thought for sure he would ask more questions, but it in the end all he said was "Well, I love your accent."

Catherine relaxed and smiled.

More and more people pressed close about them.

"Let's take a walk," Riley suggested.

So as not to be separated from him in the crowd, she kept a tight hold on his arm. His biceps was hard beneath her fingers. Almost as an afterthought, he slid his hand over top of hers, his skin warm and secure against hers.

They made their way away from the mass and walked

among the vendors selling aeronautic paraphernalia of every imaginable kind.

"Some people are really into flying," she observed.

"True hobbyists are very serious about their pursuit," he said. "No matter what the pastime."

"And what's your hobby?"

They had left the largest part of the crowd, but Catherine continued to walk alongside him with her hand curled into the crook of his arm.

"I haven't had time for a hobby," he said. "I've spent years focused on my schooling. And I just finished up my residency."

"Too busy pursuing your education and your career." She nodded. "It's understandable that you wouldn't have a hobby."

"How about you?" he asked. "What do you do with your leisure time?

"Leisure time?" She grinned. "I don't allow myself much of that. It makes me feel worthless. But I do have a passion, of sorts. I work with troubled kids. I like to get them young. The younger, the better. I mentor them, talk to them, spend time with them."

"You do social work."

The keen interest lighting his handsome face filled her with pure, unadulterated pleasure.

She couldn't help thinking that he wouldn't be so impressed with the story behind her community service work, and she sure as heck didn't want him to know that part of her history.

"I think that's admirable," he said.

"Thanks." A strange bout of shyness rolled over her.

"So, is that what you went to school to study? Social services? Psychology?"

Catherine felt the urge to squirm. "I hate to admit this, but I'm a liberal arts major."

Riley's sexy mouth quirked. "Liberal arts, huh? I have to admit to teasing the LAs I attended college with. I predicted that their future career would consist of asking me if I wanted fries with my burger."

She nodded. "Yeah, I receive the same kind of razzing, and it's okay." She shrugged. "I wanted to know a little bit of everything, and since I knew I wouldn't be allowed to have a career, I felt I might as well study whatever I…"

The bewilderment drawing his brows together made the rest of her sentence trail off into oblivion.

"Wouldn't be allowed to have a career?" he asked. "I don't understand."

Six

If nothing else, this vacation getaway was teaching Catherine that she was absolutely no good at covert operations. She couldn't tell a decent lie to save her soul. And she was pretty lousy at keeping secrets, too.

Although she hadn't meant to, she'd certainly let her loose tongue talk her into a corner here. Now to get out of this fix. But how was she going to explain to Riley that a career was impossible for her, that the events of her life—what people she'd associate with, which schools she'd attend—were planned even before her birth, without revealing her royal status to him?

When she didn't speak up right away, he said, "I've figured out that you're not like the rest of us. Well, I guess I should say not like the majority of us. You come from—" He stopped walking and turned to face her. Softly he asked,

"How do I put this without offending you? You come from privilege. Money.

"I've also figured out," he continued, "that, for some reason, you're trying to escape all that while you're here in Portland. That's why I haven't asked a bunch of questions about where you're from. Although I would love to know more about that accent of yours. But, Catherine, I don't care how wealthy your family is, it just isn't right that they should dictate to you what you will or will not do with your life. Your life is your own to live however you want to live it."

He seemed sincerely indignant on her behalf and that made a knot of emotion rise in her throat.

"I appreciate everything you've said." The words came out rusty-sounding. "More than you can know." She sighed. "But it's…" She frowned, biting her bottom lip. Then she finished with, "So damned complicated."

But it wasn't complicated, really. In fact, it was quite simple. If you're born a princess, you're expected to do certain things, act a certain way, live a certain life.

If you're not ambitious, then you spend your days indulging your every whim. You marry, and in Catherine's case her father was insisting on that sooner rather than later. And you produce royal offspring, babies to perpetuate the royal lineage.

If you choose to do something useful, you find an outlet, and hopefully, you're able to help others.

At that moment, Riley did the most extraordinary thing. He reached up and slid his fingertips along her jaw, cupped her chin in the V between his index finger and thumb. His gaze darkened with an ultraconcentrated intensity. "I'm sure it is complicated," he said gently. "Just try to remember, you do have a choice."

For an instant, Catherine felt as if no one else on earth existed except her and Riley. She stared up at him, mesmerized. Her thinking went foggy, and something happened inside. Her heart gave a little hitch that was almost painful, and some mysterious sensation made her feel light as air. It was like nothing she'd ever felt before in her life.

However, before she'd had the chance to ponder the emotions rocketing through her like some amazing stunt flyer, Riley asked, "You hungry?"

The haze in her head cleared and she realized she was starving. She nodded.

"Let's go find something to eat," he said.

At the far end of the airfield, they entered a large tented area. Delicious scents floated on the air, savory and rich, sharp and sour, and her stomach growled in a most unladylike way. She clapped a hand over her stomach in an effort to mask the rumble, but realized it was too late when Riley laughed.

He ordered two hot dogs and two iced teas, and then paid the man behind the counter.

The sandwich he handed to her seemed gargantuan. Mimicking Riley, Catherine slathered the hot dog with mustard and relish.

"This smells heavenly," she said, and then took a bite.

"That's because it's been fire roasted," he told her. "That's the only way to cook a hot dog, if you ask me. It makes them crispy on the outside and juicy on the inside."

They ate, and Catherine had to smile when Riley used his paper napkin to wipe mustard from her chin.

The sound of a loud, puttering exhaust pipe forced them to take their meal back out into the sunshine so they wouldn't miss the next aerobatic act. The stunt flyers performed a mock battle.

"That's a P-51," Riley told her. "And I think the other plane is a replica of a Japanese Zero."

At first, one pilot seemed to take the upper hand, but soon the other retaliated with several fiercely executed moves that raised a cheer from the crowd.

"How can you tell?" she asked. "Both of those planes look the same to me. Except for the exterior paint, that is."

"Oh, I think many boys—and little girls, I would imagine—go through an airplane-crazy phase." He tossed his wadded napkin into a nearby trashcan. "I was desperate to be a pilot, oh, I'd say for all of three or four weeks. That was just before I wanted to study dinosaur bones when I grew up, and just after I wanted to be a cowboy."

"I'll bet you were a cute kid," Catherine surmised. With those dark eyes, he was probably a beautiful baby, too. "So when did you decide you wanted to become a doctor?"

He went still and something troublesome tightened his features. "Not soon enough."

She waited expectantly for him to elaborate on the cryptic response, but he didn't. Instead, he took the focus off himself by asking her, "If you could have a career—any career—what would it be?"

"I'd have to say social work," she told him. She didn't have to think about it. Her volunteer work back home was about the only thing in her life that inspired her, that made her feel worthy. "I'm already deeply involved with underprivileged children. The only reason I can't call it a career is because I don't get paid for what I do."

She could tell that the mere idea irked him.

"Just because you don't need the money," he said, "doesn't mean you shouldn't be paid for your time and your effort. And for your talent."

"Oh, now, I never said I had any talent." Feeling uncomfortable with where the conversation was headed, Catherine wiped her mouth and then dropped her napkin into the can. "That was absolutely delicious," she told Riley.

A teasing glint flashed in his eyes. "At least," he murmured, "you can now say you've had an American hot dog."

She loved that mysterious heat that could swirl the air between them in the time span of a single heartbeat.

"Of one sort, anyway." Without conscious thought, her tone throbbed with a smoky sensuality that was unmistakable.

Riley's chuckle was rich, languorous, and Catherine knew she should feel mortified that the words had come out of her mouth.

"I want you to know," she hastily pressed, "that I don't normally talk this way. Or act this way."

"What way is that?"

Although his tone sounded innocent, she knew he was teasing her.

"Well, you know," she hedged, awkwardly. "I've been very…flirty. But it's not me. It's you."

"Ah, go ahead. Blame me."

She gave him a little shove. "You know what I mean. You bring it out in me. You make me outrageously brazen."

"I wouldn't call it outrageous."

The space between them suddenly became sweltering.

"I think it's cute," he murmured. Then he added, "Extremely alluring, actually. And if I'm the cause, then I'm proud to take the blame."

His willingness to shoulder all the responsibility for her abnormal behavior so charmed her that she reached up on tiptoe and gave him an impulsive kiss on the cheek.

The wonderful playful mood between the two of them continued for the remainder of the sunny afternoon.

If anyone had told Catherine that she would attend a loud, crowded aeronautic show at a very small airport where she would thoroughly enjoy herself, she'd have believed them to be ridiculously insane and out of touch with what she thought of as fun. But she was enjoying herself even among all the noise and the dust and the people.

That was when she realized that the important element wasn't so much where she was as whom she was with.

Ah, yes. The "whom" was a very important element, indeed. And it seemed that Riley was becoming a more important element of influence to her happiness with each day that passed.

A few days later, Catherine walked out of the clinic's changing room with a bounce in her step. She'd lost a couple of pounds since arriving in Portland, and she really felt the trainer working with her in the gym had developed a weight routine that was firming and defining her muscles. She felt fit. She felt good. She felt…eye-catching.

She chuckled to herself as she turned the corner, plowing right into Riley.

"Whoa!"

He caught her up against his chest, and immediately she was enveloped in the warm, male scent that was his alone.

"And what, may I ask, is so funny?" he said.

"Nothing." Revealing her conceited thoughts would surely make her look big-headed.

Another thing that had her feeling so good was Riley. They'd been spending a lot of time together. They'd had dinner every evening, gone to a movie, visited a gallery open house. He came up with something new to do each evening.

Although he tossed round the word friend an awful lot

during their fun and flirty dates, the sensuous heat that swirled between them was impossible to ignore. Well, it had been impossible for her to ignore. Riley, on the other hand, was doing rather well at it. He hadn't kissed her again, but had ended each date with an awkward hug or handshake. But he was wearing down. Catherine could tell.

She said, "I'm glad I ran into you. I'd like to take you to dinner. Someplace fancy. I want to get dressed to the nines. What's the name of Portland's most expensive restaurant?"

"Hands down, that would be La Grenouille Dorée. I'd love to go, but—"

"Wonderful," she blurted, cutting him off before he could decline. Why was his response to her and her ideas so darned important to her? "And since I'm doing the inviting, the evening is on me."

"I can't allow you to do that."

"Of course, you can," she told him. "I'm inviting you out to dinner. I can't insist on going to the best place in town and then expect you to pay for it. I want to treat."

"La Grenouille Dorée is a very fancy place," he told her, "and a bit too much for my wallet. But my ego couldn't handle your paying for everything. I'll go, but only if we split the cost. How's that?"

Anticipation strummed through her body. "Dutch treat. I can handle that. Can we meet at the restaurant?" she said, wanting to make a heart-stopping impression on him with the dress she had in mind. "And to appease that male ego of yours, I'll make the reservation in your name. Eight o'clock?" Not waiting for an answer, she started off toward the exit, calling over her shoulder, "And don't you dare be late."

* * *

Carrie Martin's feet were killing her. The temporary job she'd landed as hostess at La Grenouille Dorée might be paying her rent and putting food in her belly during her stay in Portland, but she sure wasn't used to being on her feet so many hours every night. You'd think she'd have gotten used to this after all these weeks, but that wasn't the case.

"Dr. Jacobs." She greeted the doctor with a bright smile as he entered the restaurant. "When I started my shift this evening, I saw your name in the reservation book. It's good to see you again."

"Hi, Carrie. I wish you'd call me Riley. That doctor stuff sounds stuffy away from the clinic." He tucked his keys into his trouser pocket. "I didn't know you worked here."

"It's just a summer job," she told him. "I teach back in San Francisco. I'll have to get myself back there very soon."

She heard the anxiety in her own voice. Apparently, Riley Jacobs heard it, too.

"No sign of him yet?"

"No," she said. She spent time every day sitting in her car in the parking lot of Richard's apartment complex watching for him. Something in Riley's expression gave the impression she could truly trust him. "Y-you really are concerned."

Uncertainty churned in her, and she wasn't sure if what she'd said came out sounding like a statement or a question.

"Of course, I'm concerned. Everyone at the clinic is worried about Dr. Richie. We want to know he's all right."

"The other day," she started, "in your office you said you wanted Richard to help in the lab. With the testing of that oil. Did you really mean that? Or do you— Does the hospital intend to get him into some kind of trouble?"

Riley truly looked confused. "Carrie, it's not as if he's broken any laws."

She lifted a shoulder. "False advertising? I don't know. I've just been worried sick that my outburst caused more problems for him than anyone is saying."

"There was nothing false about the advertising he gave NoWait. People have lost weight. That's what Richard said people could expect. And that's what the oil provided." Riley's mouth twitched. "How could he know that NoWait also offers some other…unexpected results?"

Carrie sighed. "You mean how it turns people into lusty Lucifers?" He didn't respond and she really hadn't expected him to. "You were serious about wanting Richard's help, then?" she asked. It was so important to her to know for certain that Richard's reputation wasn't in jeopardy because of something she'd said or done. Yes, her ex-husband had invented the darned oil, but she'd knocked over the first explosive domino that day in his seminar.

"We're very serious," he told her. "And we need him soon, Carrie. The testing is getting underway with or without him. Hospital administration is pushing hard. But I think it's imperative that he be there from the get-go. I don't know how much longer I can hold off the testing."

The agony she felt was reflected on her face, she was sure. "We've got two employees out sick, so I've been pulling double shifts here this week. I've had no time to really look for Richard, although I have stalked his apartment for a while each day. But even if I had the time, I don't know where else to look."

Riley seemed to stare at her, unseeing. His brow creased

with a thought. "When you knew Richard before," he asked, "when the two of you were married, what kinds of things did he like to do? Where did he enjoy hanging out? When I'm upset, I always go to the Chinese Gardens here in town. Did Richard have a certain place he'd hole up when he was young? A place that might have helped him to think?"

Her half-hearted laugh contained no humor. "Nearly twenty years have come and gone since we were married."

He nodded. "Think about it, though. You might come up with something. He's got to be somewhere."

"That he does." She sighed again. "I see you requested a table for two. Should I seat you now, or would you like to wait in the bar?"

"I'll wait at the table, thanks."

Carrie nodded, reaching for two menus. "Right this way, then."

Deep trouble. That was what Riley realized he was in the moment Catherine entered the dining room. And he was in it up to his waist. No, up to his neck.

The interior of La Grenouille Dorée could easily be spotlighted in *Architectural Digest,* or some fancy interior design magazine. The cut-crystal chandeliers reflected the light in small splashes of prismatic color. The rich wood paneling covering the walls had an old-world beauty. The carpet underfoot was plush enough to sink into.

It was one of Portland's classiest spots. And Catherine fitted in as if she'd been born right, smack-dab in the middle of these lavish surroundings.

First off, she walked in as if she owned the place. Her head was held high, her shoulders square. And the dress she wore knocked the damned breath out of him.

She looked hot in red. The fabric looked almost slick, the sheen inviting a man to reach out and smooth his fingertips against it. However, there was nowhere that he could touch that would have been safe.

The dress was an off-the-shoulder getup. A sheath, he thought the fashion industry would call it. The dress hugged her body in a way that actually had him feeling downright jealous.

Her shoes were narrow wisps of leather strapping ultra-high heels to her dainty feet. The tips of her toes, her fingernails, even her evening purse were the same shade of cherry as the rest of her outfit. Riley saw quite a few heads turn when Catherine made her entrance.

"You look lovely," he said, standing and offering her a quick kiss on the cheek. He wanted to say more, do more, but he was keeping his libido and all the urges brimming from it under strict control.

Catherine smiled. "Thank you, Riley."

She knew she looked good, and the poise she displayed, that confidence, was extremely alluring to him.

Looking around him, though, at the opulent surroundings and at the almost too-beautiful woman sitting across from him, Riley quickly found his own confidence waning. A bout of insecurity set in, and as the evening progressed, the feeling refused to budge.

The abundant choices on the menu made him nervous, but Catherine wasn't daunted in the least.

She suggested they begin their meal with an aperitif, and when he shot her a look of bewilderment, she explained that the Lillet listed on the menu was a light predinner drink made from a blend of wine, brandy, fruits and herbs and was thought to stimulate the appetite.

Something had him suggesting that she go ahead and

order their meals for them, and she didn't hesitate accepting what she evidently took as an exciting challenge.

A mild intimidation set in when Catherine rattled off the foreign names of the wines offered as if she'd personally visited each and every country of origin. Whether the wine was French, Italian, German—even Russian—she confidently pronounced the name to the wine steward. The two of them discussed vintage, producer, body, aroma.

Riley had never thought of himself as a country bumpkin. Portland was a great city in which to be born and raised. In the past, when he'd heard people talk in what he would judge as esoteric jargon, Riley had silently snickered at their pomposity. However, he didn't detect a single ounce of arrogance in Catherine throughout the process of choosing a pre-dinner drink, or appetizer, entrée, wine or anything else for that matter. She was simply intent on ordering the food and drink that would make their evening most pleasurable.

Several times Riley resisted the urge to loosen his necktie and give himself some breathing room. He'd been much more comfortable carting a mustard-slathered hot dog around at the airport last weekend.

It was clear, however, that tonight Catherine was in her element.

Trouble was, she'd also been in her element while they were sharing grilled hot dogs and watching airplanes do spirals in the sky.

This woman was a contradiction…and she was the most intriguing person he'd ever met.

The waiter cleared their table of china and cutlery, slipping away in well-trained silence.

Catherine's contented sigh drew Riley's attention.

"How about a digestif?" she asked. "I'm too full for dessert, but a pousse-café would be very nice, don't you think?" Before Riley could respond, the waiter appeared and Catherine made her request.

Riley frowned, not because he hadn't a clue what she'd just suggested—which he hadn't—and not because he was the least put out that she'd ordered for him, but because the question whispering across his brain became so damned vexing that he couldn't keep himself from voicing it.

"What is it you're looking for, Catherine?"

The pleasure that had relaxed her features just a moment before wilted and she suddenly looked pensive.

"What do you mean?"

"From me," he said. "From your trip to Portland."

Up until now, he'd tried to respect her privacy. He'd taken her out to eat, shown her his city and, he hoped, provided her a good time. All without asking a lot of personal questions. Because that was what he thought she wanted. Because she'd led him to believe from the very first that she was hiding from something or someone and she didn't want to be questioned. But, for some reason, tonight's experience had simply put Riley over the top and he could remain silent no longer.

When she didn't respond, he continued, "I don't mean any offense, Catherine. Honestly, I don't. I told you at the air show that I've realized some things about you. About your…circumstances. I've tried not to ask a lot of questions. I thought that I understood that you're trying to escape from something. And I'd thought that something might be a…well, a certain lifestyle. That you were looking for—I don't know—something simpler. Something more down to earth. You said you wanted to be 'ordinary.'" He felt he wasn't explaining himself very well. "That you wanted to experience the life of a normal Joe.

"But tonight…" Riley paused. He felt as if he were digging a hole for himself, that he was about to say something that just might hurt Catherine's feelings, and he certainly didn't want to do that. But this experience tonight had ripped him out of his own element—his own comfortable world—and had plunked him down in an overt lavishness that made him very uncomfortable.

"Tonight, what?" she prompted him. "I'd like to know what's on your mind. I want you to feel free to say whatever it is you want to say."

There was no turning back, he realized.

"I feel as if you dragged me into your world," he said plainly. There, it was out. "And I'm confused because this kind of—I don't know—extravagance is what I thought you wanted to escape. But you've enjoyed yourself this evening. With aperitifs and *bocconcini Fiorentina*—" he knew he'd hacked up the pronunciation, but he plowed ahead "—and pousse-café—"

As if right on cue, the waiter brought cups of dark-brewed coffee that were accompanied by tiny glasses of some thick, current-hued cordial.

Troubled shadows crept into her beautiful blue eyes.

Riley attempted to chuckle but didn't quite succeed. "I mean, you have to admit that this is a far cry from hot dogs at Hillsboro Airport."

She sat up straight, leaned forward and reached out to touch the sleeve of his dinner jacket.

"Riley, I never meant to make you feel—"

"No, no," he assured her, suddenly desperate for her not to put a name to the emotion raging through him. "I've had a good time tonight. I have. Just watching you has been quite an experience." He paused long enough to swallow. "But, Catherine, it's so obvious to me that you belong here. In this kind of setting, this kind of atmosphere. That you truly enjoy this kind of thing. That you've done it a thousand times before, and that you plan to do it a thousand times more. And that leads me to believe that I had it all wrong. That I had you all wrong. And if that's so," he said, shaking his head, "then it brings me back to my original question: What are you looking for? Why are you in Portland? Why are you with me?"

The expression on her beautiful face was inscrutable.

"I'm a regular Joe, Catherine," he said. "Just as regular as they come. My parents were working-class people. For thirty years, my dad drove a forklift for a warehouse right here in Portland. And he worked a second job that was just as blue-collar. Mom was a part-time checkout clerk at a grocery store. She quit working when I was born, but then went back to her old job as soon as I started school.

"I was damned lucky to get into college," he pressed on. For more reasons than money, he thought. But she didn't have to know that. "And I graduated up to my ears in debt. I haven't really been anywhere. I haven't experienced much. I'm not suave or sophisticated or the least bit worldly." He stopped and leveled his gaze on her. "I guess I'm just a little confused about why an obvious debutante like you would want to hang out with a hot-dog-and-soda kind of guy like me."

The whole room seemed to go very still. Maybe the restaurant had been quiet all along and Riley simply hadn't noticed it.

The longer Catherine was silent and staring, the more his curiosity grew.

She relaxed in her seat and consciously inhaled deeply. He got the impression that she was gathering up her courage to reveal all.

However, before she could speak, Carrie Martin approached the table.

"I'm so sorry to bother you," she said, directing her apology at Catherine before turning her attention to Riley.

Although this wasn't the greatest moment, Riley introduced the two women, and Catherine told Carrie, "I've seen you at the clinic."

Carrie nodded. "I try to drop by every day." She once again directed her gaze at Riley. She wrung her hands, her agitation evident as she told Riley, "I came to thank you for what you said when you arrived."

Taken aback, he went over their conversation in his head, trying to remember what he'd said to her.

"I told you I didn't know where to look for Richard," she reminded him. "And you told me to think about when I knew him before." Her eyes danced. "I hadn't thought to do that before. And now I know where to look for him. Or I think I do, anyway."

"That's great. Really."

More hand-wringing. "I wanted to let you know that I'll tell him to come see you."

"That would be wonderful," he told her. "And I want you to know it's going to be all right for him. Everyone at the clinic is interested in his work. You can tell him I said so."

"I will, Riley." She backed away. "Thank you again."

He smiled, and she turned away.

Looking across the table at Catherine, Riley said, "Carrie is Richard Strong's ex-wife. He was a mainstay of the clinic before your arrival. He was better known as Dr. Richie."

"I read about him in the newspaper."

"He left the Healthy Living Clinic suddenly and hasn't

been in touch with anyone since. Carrie hopes to find him."
He glanced in the direction Carrie had gone. "I hope she
does. We could use his help at the clinic."

He lifted his gaze back to Catherine. Softly he said, "I'm
sorry for the interruption. We should drink our coffee before it gets cold."

He reached for the cream pitcher, but Catherine stopped
him by taking his hand.

"I need to tell you something, Riley."

Something in her tone made him lace his fingers with
hers. She seemed to need some support.

"You're right," she hesitantly began. "There are certain…aspects of my life that I'm trying to escape. But I—
I—" She stammered to a stop, seemingly unsure of exactly
how to phrase her thoughts.

"Please try to understand," she tried again, "that I do
have what I think are very good reasons for remaining se-
cretive about what I'm going through."

He nodded. So she wasn't going to tell him what he
wanted to know. He didn't like secrets, but he knew the im-
portance of them. He had a few of his own. He could see
the relief sweeping through her, easing her tense facial
muscles.

"As for why I want to be with you…"

Her head dipped timidly, and Riley felt something in his
gut tighten.

"I like you, Riley. I enjoy being with you. And I think
you enjoy being with me. Can't that be enough?"

With her free hand, she picked up the crystal cordial
glass, lifting it several inches.

"To friends."

Riley studied her face—each feature classic and lovely.
The Catherine he'd come to know was a strong woman.

But there was a fragility there, as well. A vulnerability that stirred in him a compulsion to protect. Even if that meant protecting her from his own curiosity.

He might not know what she was running from. But at this moment in time, she certainly wasn't asking too much of him, was she?

The crystal was cool against his fingertips as he raised his glass and touched the rim to hers.

"To friends."

Seven

"Mom, are you sure this is what you want to do?"

Carrie Martin listened to the sound of her son's voice as it crackled over the cell phone. Since the death of his stepfather, Jason had become overly protective of her, and it warmed Carrie's heart to hear the concern in his tone.

He continued, "I don't like the idea of you driving around Portland at all hours of the night."

"Honey, you know I work late at the restaurant," she said. "I'm out driving nearly every night, anyway."

"Yes," Jason balked, "but around pool halls? They're not much different from bars, really. And if you're going to search out all the places with pool tables, you'll have to go into quite a few bars. People drinking and smoking. Loud music and fights breaking out."

Her "mother's antenna" perked right up. "And just how do you know that?" she asked pointedly. "You're only nineteen, Jason. You haven't been going out to bars with your friends, have you?"

He gave a long-suffering sigh. "You know me better than that."

And she did. Carrie smiled as she cradled the telephone next to her ear. Her son was a good kid.

"You really think you'll find him playing pool somewhere?" he asked.

Carrie was worried that Jason hadn't called Richard anything except "him" and "he" since she'd told her son she intended to come to Portland in search of his father.

"You can call him your dad, you know."

"Can I?" Jason asked. "Can we be sure how he's going to react to that?"

Jason had a point. She had no idea how Richard would react to the news that he had a son.

"Doesn't change the fact that he's your father. Getting back to the original topic," she said, "I have no idea if I'll find him shooting pool. But I can't think of any place else to look."

After a moment, her son said, "You never told me he liked to shoot pool."

The slight accusation edging Jason's words roused feelings of guilt in Carrie. "There never really seemed a proper time to talk about—"

"I know," he said, gently cutting her off. "I'm sorry. I shouldn't have said it like that. I just…I'm curious, you know?"

It was completely natural for a young man to be curious about the father he'd never met. Why hadn't Carrie opened up this subject before? Her guilt grew like the mammoth, inky Blob from that dreadful science-fiction movie.

"When your father was upset," she told her son, "he used to spend hours and hours playing pool. It was a relief valve for him, I guess." Her voice softened as she remembered, "He was quite good, as I recall."

The line went quiet for quite some time, and then Jason asked, "You're sure you want to go through with this? With finding him, I mean? You don't have to, you know. You can always just go back to San Francisco and act as if this summer never happened."

"I can't, honey. I've made a complete mess of things here for Richard. I have to fix it. At the very least, I have to try. I really need to explain things to him."

How she would do that was beyond her, though. The feelings raging through her were conflicting to the highest degree. Her anger over how they had parted waged a constant war with the sympathy she felt for her ex-husband, with the heartwarming memory of the good times they'd shared so many years ago.

"And you're really going to tell him about me?" Jason asked.

Her son's question expressed hope…and a terrific trepidation.

"He deserves to know. And you deserve for him to know."

"What do you think he'll say? What do you think he'll do? Do you think he'll want to—"

Carrie stopped him, "Jason, I don't have answers to any of those questions. I have to find him first."

After a moment of silence, he asked, "You'll call me?"

"You know I will."

"Love you, Mom."

"I love you, too, honey."

Carrie snapped the cell phone closed and slipped it into

her purse. The lights illuminating the restaurant's parking lot cast a yellow glow in her car's interior. She'd worked long and hard tonight. All she wanted to do was go home, soak in a hot tub and then hit the hay.

But her conscience wouldn't let her.

She stared down at the list of pool halls she'd copied out of the telephone book. The names of at least a dozen businesses were printed on the slip of paper she held. Visiting them all tonight would be impossible. But she could check out at least two of them. Maybe even three.

If the other employees returned to work tomorrow, as planned, she might even be able to leave a little early.

Carrie started the engine of her car and backed out of the parking space. She felt optimistic that she'd find Richard. But what would she say to him once she did?

What is it you're looking for?

Riley's words echoed through Catherine's head as she lay on the bed, wide-awake and staring at the ceiling.

Of course, she had known that the conversations they'd had, the clues and innuendoes she'd offered him, would have him guessing about her circumstances.

I've tried not to ask a lot of questions.

She slid her hand over her stomach, the silk of her nightgown cool against her palm, and she smiled. Riley was probably the nicest guy she'd ever met in her life. Of course, he was curious about how she came to be in Portland. It was only natural that he was wondering, yet he'd refrained from asking her questions.

I understood that you're trying to escape from something.

Oh, but Riley had no idea just how badly she'd love to escape the fate that life had handed her. However, there was no escape. She couldn't evade reality forever. She knew that. This vacation might offer a short reprieve. But walking down the aisle—to meet a man of her father's choosing, a man she didn't know and didn't love—would be inevitable.

So what was she looking for? Why had she gotten on that plane in Lextanya? Why had she flown thousands of miles across the ocean to Portland, Oregon, where she knew no one and no one knew her?

She'd told herself she wanted a little naughty fun. So why was she so willing simply to spend time with Riley? Why was she so willing to let their relationship progress on its own?

Catherine rolled over onto her side, plumped up the pillow and tried to get comfortable, but the discomfort she felt had little to do with the firmness of the mattress or the softness of the bed linens.

Restlessly, she flopped over onto her back and stared again at the faint shadows on the smooth white ceiling.

She'd told Riley she wanted to spend time with him because she liked him. And that was the honest truth of the matter.

The truth was that she was desperate to be liked.

That sounded damned pathetic to her.

But as pathetic as it sounded, could that be the real reason she'd left Lextanya? So that she could find some friends, people who liked her, who enjoyed being around her simply because of the kind of person she was.

Not because she was wealthy. Not because she was a princess. Not because her last name happened to be von Husden. Not because—

The jangling of the bedside phone startled a gasp out of her.

Reaching over, she picked up the receiver and offered a tentative greeting.

"Cat, I'd like to know just how long this little escapade of yours is going to continue."

The sound of her father's voice struck her mute.

"It's time for you to come home," he said.

Uttering the profane phrase that ricocheted in her brain would have been inexcusable. Her father might be stuffy and insufferable, but he was still her father and he deserved her respect.

She was finally able to work her tongue and ask, "How did you find me?"

His harsh chuckle grated across the phone line. "Don't be silly, Cat. You used your credit card at a dress shop. Granted, there was only one purchase, but that was enough to have you tracked down. You should know you can't hide from me. Not for long, anyway. You're not smart enough to outwit me."

Wasn't that the truth? She was quickly learning she wasn't smart enough to outwit anyone, and she only got herself into trouble when she tried.

Stifling a groan, Catherine thought back to when she might have slipped up. She'd been so careful to use cash to pay for everything. It must have been during her shopping excursion with Faye. The two of them had chattered like chipmunks all day long. She guessed she'd become preoccupied and had pulled out her card without thinking. Even now she couldn't remember in which store she'd used it.

"Father, I've truly been enjoying myself. I need more time. I want to savor a little more of this vacation."

"But your whole life has been a vacation."

She bristled at his words. She'd done some really good

work with the needy children of Lextanya. Why couldn't he recognize her contribution?

"Come home," he ordered.

"I will not."

"Cat—"

"At least, not yet."

Tension shimmered in the silence that followed.

"Father, I know what is required of me. I understand everything that you expect. And I know I must return home. Eventually."

She feared that her voice quivered with the unexpected emotions that seemed to well up from nowhere—anxiety, despair, desperation. However, if her father detected what she was feeling, he didn't acknowledge it.

"You promised to come home. Your sister has been very patient and—"

"Please." She cut him off, her tone rising slightly. "Just a little more time." She pressed her lips together, attempting to garner control. Her voice was small as she pleaded, "I'm not asking for much." Catherine swallowed the tears threatening to spill. She wouldn't cry. "Please, Father."

The stillness became nerve-racking, but she was determined not to say another word. She needed to win this small battle of wills. It wasn't as if she were asking the world. She feared she sounded farcical. Yvonne was the one who usually resorted to melodrama. But Catherine felt desperate.

"One week. Please give me one more week."

Her plea met with silence.

Finally, her father said, "You may have till the weekend. I have big plans then. There will be a party on Saturday evening, honoring you and Étienne. Your engagement will be announced at Sunday's formal luncheon. I'm looking at flight schedules now. There's one leaving Portland at midnight Friday. A ticket will be waiting at the gate for you. Be on that plane, Cat."

The line went dead.

With a trembling hand, Catherine replaced the receiver in its cradle. She exhaled, unaware that she'd even been holding her breath.

She hated that her father could make her feel like a frightened six-year-old. His cowering Fat Cat. A terrified child who, desperately wanting her father's love and attention, had silently suffered his taunts and teasing. Heckling that, like strong acid, had ultimately corroded away every semblance of her self-esteem.

No wonder she'd wanted to slip out of her royal persona. She didn't much like Cat von Husden. The oldest von Husden princess was weak and had no confidence whatsoever.

Catherine Houston was another story altogether. She walked with her head held high. She'd made friends who really cared about her.

She thought of Faye Lassen. They had become fast friends. Faye had even taken Catherine's advice on wardrobe and makeup and hairstyle because Faye trusted Catherine's sense of style.

Helping Faye to break out of her shell made Catherine feel pretty damned good. Simply knowing Faye was her friend made her feel good, too.

Then there was Riley.

I'm just a regular Joe.

His description of himself at dinner tonight whispered through her head.

A regular Joe was just what she'd been looking for in a friend.

Catherine slid down onto the mattress and pulled the sheet up to her chin.

Who was she kidding? She wasn't looking for a friend.

She wanted a regular Joe to like her, yes. But she wanted much more from Riley than that.

Images of Riley—with his dark good looks, intelligent smile and quick wit—passed through her thoughts. Then she thought of Étienne. The man her father wanted her to marry might be handsome, but no amount of striking features could make up for a deficient character.

At twenty-six, she was looking down a long, loveless road if she respected her father's wishes. Absently, her hand slid down the cool, cotton sheet, over the swell of her breast, coming to rest on her flat tummy.

A loveless, passion-less road.

Many a von Husden had traveled it. And most of them had survived. Many of them had even succeeded in finding some semblance of satisfaction in their lives. They had learned to be content with their lot.

Could she get her mind-set to the place it needed to be in order to be content with her lot?

She closed her eyes, surprised to feel a single hot tear roll from the corner and slip down her temple.

I'm a regular Joe.

Again, Riley's words resonated in her head.

She did want more from Riley than mere friendship. She had to force herself to ponder the idea, to grasp it, to twist and turn it over in her mind and truly examine the idea.

She wanted Riley—a regular Joe who was ignorant of her true identity—to know her, to like her....

To want her.

Thursday found Catherine racing on the treadmill, sweat dampening her brow and underarms. She felt as though she'd been in a pressure cooker since taking that call from her father, and each sunrise only seemed to bring the strain of more steam.

She was running out of time!

The gym was turning out to be a great release valve for her. Physical exertion released endorphins that gave her a runner's high. She felt good, at least for a little while. And the exercise helped to clear her mind so she could think better.

Gazing across the workout room, Catherine spied some unusual activity between a trainer who was fairly new at the clinic and a male client who was lifting weights.

The trainer, an attractive young woman, was acting as the man's spotter. He was flat on his back as he struggled to extend the weight bar to a full press. What Catherine found so curious was that the trainer didn't seem the least bit interested in her job as spotter. Instead, the woman was bending over the man, smoothing her hands over the muscles of his chest.

Catherine stepped off the treadmill, automatically reaching for the towel that was draped over her shoulders. She wiped the perspiration from her forehead, noticing that several others in the gym were casting surreptitious glances at the couple across the room. Catherine stifled a grin at the trainer's overtly sexual behavior. If the woman kept that up, men would be flocking to the Healthy Living Clinic to work out.

Just then Faye pushed her way through the swinging door. She waved and smiled, making a beeline for Catherine.

Catherine's jaw dropped with surprise.

Faye's dark hair had been cut in a fresh style, and she wore another new outfit, a bright turquoise dress that looked quite striking on her trim figure. Faye had stopped wearing those white lab jackets. And there was something else about her, something Catherine couldn't quite put her finger on.

"Hey, there," Faye greeted.

"Your glasses!" The words burst from Catherine's throat. "You're not wearing them."

Faye seemed all too pleased that Catherine had noticed. Her tone dropped to a conspiratorial level as she revealed, "Contacts. I saw my optometrist yesterday afternoon."

"Your eyes are so blue!" Catherine tried to keep her amazement under control, but it was next to impossible.

Color flushed Faye's cheeks, making her all the more stunning.

"My goodness, woman!" Catherine exclaimed. "I thought you were beautiful with just a new outfit, but now that I can see your eyes, you're Miss Universe material."

Faye had the good sense to laugh. "Cut that out. I am not. I'm too old to be a 'Miss' anything."

Catherine circled her, looking at her friend from all angles. "But you do have to admit—" she enlisted a sexy accent "—you look marvelous."

Again, Faye grinned. "I wouldn't be a good judge of that, but I can tell you that I sure feel marvelous."

"If this doesn't help get you noticed," Catherine observed, "nothing will."

A grimace wrinkled Faye's nose. "As I've already said, I'd like to be noticed for my skill as a doctor. And for all the work I continue to put into this place. But if my new look accomplishes the task," she said with a shrug, "I'll just have to be satisfied, won't I?"

The women shared a laugh.

Faye said, "I came to ask you if we were still on for

lunch tomorrow. I don't want you leaving town without saying goodbye."

Catherine had told Faye right away that she would be returning home Friday night. "I wouldn't miss it, Faye."

"Well, I have tons to do—"

"Can I ask you a question? Do you know where Riley is?"

"He's attending a conference over at the hospital."

Disappointment rounded Catherine's shoulders. "He mentioned that he had meetings, but…"

Faye told her, "It's a two-day event."

"Well, hell's bells." Frustration got the better of Catherine.

Her friend's low whistle had her lifting her gaze.

"Someone's got it bad." Faye's finely shaped eyebrows arched high.

Across the room, the weight bar clattered loudly into its metal cradle. Several people squealed in surprise and others gave a startled jump, but collectively, all eyes turned in the direction of the racket.

The female trainer had straddled the man lying on the weight bench, their kiss deep and obviously thorough.

Catherine couldn't stop her open grin.

Faye gasped.

A few titters and snickers echoed off the gym's high ceiling.

"Diane!" Faye's tone was sharp.

The young trainer's head lifted. Her lips glistened and her eyes were glazed with desire. The man lying prone looked up, too. His expression seemed groggy, as if he'd just been jarred from a deep sleep and was unsure of where he was and what was going on.

Catherine actually pressed her fingers against her mouth to keep from chuckling.

"May I speak to you, Diane?" Faye said. When the woman didn't immediately react, Faye stressed, "Now!"

Diane actually blinked several times. Then she glanced down at the man she'd just kissed, and when her gaze swung back to Faye, her eyes were wide. She lifted her leg over the man, pressing her hand against his chest for balance.

"Mr. Hollister," Faye said, "you should probably come along, too."

The man shoved himself to a stand and followed on Diane's heels.

Faye said to Catherine, "Would you excuse me for a moment?"

"No problem." Catherine hooked the towel around her neck. "I'm off to the shower. I'll catch you in a bit."

Faye nodded, and Catherine trotted off down the hallway leading to the locker rooms.

The latch felt hard and cold in Catherine's grasp. She tossed her towel in the wide-mouthed laundry bin and then turned to pull her duffel bag from the locker. After only a moment, she heard Faye's voice and realized that she'd brought Diane and Mr. Hollister down the hallway to talk. They must have been standing right outside the door of the women's locker room.

"Have you lost your minds?" Faye asked. "I don't know what's going on between the two of you, but—"

"Nothing's going on." Anxiety painted every syllable of the man's urgent response. "I'm a married man. A happily married man. My wife is going to kill me if she finds out about—"

"She won't find out." Diane sounded frantic. "Why would anyone want to cause problems for you, Mr. Hollister?" Her tone grew humble as she added, "I'm awfully sorry. I—I don't know what happened. You have to believe me. You, too, Dr. Lassen. I just don't understand it. One minute I was standing there spotting, the next I was…well, I was—"

"I witnessed what you were doing," Faye said.

Catherine shouldn't be eavesdropping, but the situation was too humorous not to.

She heard Faye nonchalantly ask, "Mr. Hollister, are you using the NoWait oil?"

"No," he told her. "I gave mine back last week. I wasn't too happy about it, either. I'd lost three pounds in three days using that stuff."

"I understand," Faye said. Switching gears drastically, she said, "Well, I think you should go home today and tell your wife exactly what happened. Tell her that your gym workouts must be working, that they've made you irresistible and that a trainer kissed you out of the blue. Tell your wife that Diane has apologized. And then assure her it won't happen again. Right, Diane?"

"Yes, ma'am," came the quick answer.

Faye continued, "Mr. Hollister, I think it would be best if your wife heard the story from you. You know how people can be. They love to gossip."

"You're probably right," the man murmured.

"I'm glad this is settled," Faye said.

Catherine shook her head at Faye's confident manner. Was there nothing that ruffled that woman?

She overheard Faye say, "Go and finish your weight training, Mr. Hollister. I'll make sure you have another spotter. Just give me a second to talk to Diane."

As he walked away, his sneakers sounded like mouse peeps against the clean tile floor.

Faye said, "Hand over the NoWait."

Catherine could imagine Faye standing there with her palm held out flat.

Diane blubbered, "B-but I only wanted to try it. It's harmless. It's just oil. And I only used a little—"

"You could lose your job over this."

"Dr. Lassen," the young woman pleaded, "I need to work. Please."

"You know we've been collecting the oil."

"Yes," Diane said. "That's what made me so curious. About the other…effects."

"We will not talk about any effects," Faye said emphatically. "If you're going to remain an employee of this clinic, I have to know that I can trust you to follow the rules and regulations. This oil was not to be used. We're allocating a huge amount of money to testing. If people start talking—"

"People are already talking."

"And that's exactly why we're taking the oil out of circulation."

After heaving a sigh, Diane said, "I'm sorry, Dr. Lassen. I was stupid to take it."

"Yes, well, hopefully the worst is over with. Now back to work. And stay away from Mr. Hollister."

Everything went quiet. Catherine wrestled her bag from the locker and unzipped it. But she couldn't even remember what she was looking for. Her mind was spinning too fast.

That trainer had been using NoWait, the weight-loss oil that had been touted by Dr. Richie when the clinic had first opened. Diane had practically devoured Mr. Hollister with that kiss of hers. And Mr. Hollister hadn't seemed to mind a bit. In fact, he'd seemed a pretty willing participant.

Suddenly, Catherine's heart was pounding.

She had two days before she had to go home. Two measly days to discover just how desirable Riley found her.

If she had more time, she was certain their friendly relationship would grow into something more. In time, she was sure she could get him to kiss her with uncontrollable passion. He liked her. He enjoyed being with her. And there were moments when a mysterious mood danced around them both. Well, she certainly felt it dancing around her.

But she needed proof that Riley felt it, too. She wanted to be sure. Positive that she had what it took to make Riley desire her without the tiara, without a vault full of money and jewels, without the von Husden reputation.

Damn it! She wanted to feel Riley's mouth on hers. She wanted to feel his fingers smoothing across her bare skin.

But time was running out!

She stared unseeing across the empty locker room.

Could NoWait be her answer?

Eight

Riley knocked on the door of Catherine's suite. Antsy and out-of-sorts, he rocked on his heels and reached to tug on the collar of his shirt.

She wasn't going to like the fact that he didn't intend to stay for the dinner she'd planned, but he had his reasons. Oh, boy, did he ever.

He hadn't actually seen Catherine since they'd shared that extravagant dinner at La Grenouille Dorée, her invitation for tonight having been left in a hand-written note with the clinic's receptionist. Yet, it felt as if he hadn't gone a single minute of the past few days without thinking about her.

It hadn't been that bad, of course, but Riley knew too much of his mental energies were focused on her. They were supposed to be friends, damn it. Friends, and nothing more.

He'd tried to blame the coordinators of the administrative conference he'd just attended. If the speakers had been livelier, more informative, more interesting, then Riley wouldn't have become plagued with boredom. He wouldn't have drifted off into daydreams of Catherine, her light and lilting laughter, her glittering blue eyes, her flirtatious grin.

Oh, that flirtatious grin.

Blaming the conference speakers hadn't been fair, really. Most all of the meetings he'd been required to attend since taking over at the clinic had been tedious at best. He simply wasn't cut out to be an administrator; he missed practicing real medicine.

But, his biggest problem had nothing to do with meetings and speakers. It had everything to do with one blond-haired beauty.

The effect she had on him was damned amazing.

The other night over their after-dinner drinks, she'd stressed that all she'd been looking for was a friend. And he'd been relieved to hear it. But this so-called friendship had him feeling lighter than air. The mere thought of her was like a fresh breeze blowing across his soul.

Riley nearly groaned. Syrupy poetics was not his style.

However, he couldn't dispute the fact that he found Catherine interesting. She made him think. She made him laugh at himself.

Remembering some of her antics had him smiling even now.

He quickly caught himself and frowned. He couldn't let this woman get under his skin. He couldn't allow their friendship to grow into anything more. He'd been doing all he could to control his feelings, his urges. And doing so was becoming more and more difficult.

That was why he intended to cut this visit short tonight. So he could keep a tight rein on their relationship and on himself.

Oh, who the hell was he trying to fool?

He had control over nothing.

He wanted her, damn it! He wanted her bad.

She sparked a blazing desire in him like no other woman he'd ever met.

He'd thought the two days he'd spent sequestered in meeting after meeting would help clear her from his mind, help him get a grip on his reaction to her. But as it turned out, not seeing her had only made him think about her more.

However, no matter how strong his physical needs, he was bound and determined not to act on them. The toughest moment of being with her was always whenever they parted company. He had an overwhelming desire to take her in his arms and kiss her soundly, but time and again he'd skipped a fast step around the moment and had succeeded in escaping with a mere hug or handshake.

He'd only kissed her once. And that had been because she'd asked him to so brazenly that he hadn't been able to refuse.

A chaste kiss that very first time they'd gone out together.

However, he could still feel her luscious lips against his. He could still smell her jasmine scent. All he had to do was close his eyes.

The front door of Catherine's suite popped open, and so did his eyelids.

"Riley! Hi. So you did get my message. Come on in."

The memory of that one, tiny kiss had so fogged his brain that he just stood there while she turned and walked away from him. His gaze latched on to the sway of her hips and automatically slid down the long length of her shapely legs. The soft aroma of her perfume drifted in her wake.

Her black skirt was short. And tight.

It wasn't until she flashed her bright smile at him that he realized she was once again facing him. Her blouse was cut low—deliciously low—and the creamy swell of her breasts mesmerized him.

"You do intend to come inside, don't you?"

Her query had a smooth, almost smoky quality to it, and her blue eyes sparkled with a bold and teasing glint. Immediately, Riley became aware of a humming undercurrent vibrating all around him.

"Riley."

He blinked. "Yes?" Again, he blinked. Step over the threshold and close the damned door! "Yes." His voice was stronger now. "Of course."

The effort he put forth was much more than the task required. He gulped in a lungful of air while still facing the door he closed.

Focus, man. You are not staying. He scrambled for excuses. You have dry cleaning to pick up. You have a sick aunt who needs a visit. You have to get to bed early because—

No, no. Do not mention *bed*. Do not even think about uttering that word!

"Riley, are you okay?"

Her silky voice so close to his ear made him jump. He hadn't been aware that she'd approached.

"Fine," he said. "I'm fine."

Evidently she anticipated his intention to back away from her and she grasped his arm with both her hands.

"Come and have some wine," she said, leaning her head

against his shoulder and coaxing him along with her into the sitting room.

Her hair brushed his jaw, and his breath hitched in his chest. He wanted to speak up. He wanted to pull away.

That wasn't quite the truth. He didn't want to do either of those things. But he knew he should do both of those things.

So why wasn't he acting on what he knew he should be doing?

"Guess what I did this afternoon."

The husky tone of her voice made his flesh come alive, and he felt he was being swept along on some wild Pacific rip current.

She pulled him down onto the couch with her, and released her hold on him long enough to pour the wine that had been breathing on the coffee table. She handed him a glass and then leaned against the couch back, snuggling up close to his arm again. He was aware of the firm roundness of her breast.

Catherine had shown herself to be a touchy-feely kind of person. She'd reach out and slide her palm over his hand during an intense conversation, or poke him on the shoulder with her finger, or give him a diminutive push to make a point. But she'd never quite been this physical before.

"Well, are you going to guess?"

"I—I can't," he confessed. Hell, he couldn't even think straight. "Really. Whatever you did, though, you seem excited about it."

"Oh, I am." She shifted her hips, and ended up even closer to him. "I visited the Boys and Girls Club. It's called Blazers and it's right here in Portland. They run programs for kids who are six to eighteen."

Energy pulsed from her, lighting up her eyes, her smile.

Lord, she was a beautiful woman. And she never failed to astonish him.

She was supposed to be on a vacation. That was what she'd called it, anyway. She could have gone on a river cruise, visited the Oaks Amusement Park or taken a winery tour. Entertainment abounded in Portland. But what had she done? She'd visited an organization that helps disadvantaged kids.

"Did you know," she continued, "that eight thousand children participate in their activities and programs. Isn't that amazing?"

What was amazing, he thought, was her.

She blushed, and he knew without a doubt that he'd never seen a woman more gorgeous than Catherine.

"Why, thank you," she whispered softly. "You're pretty amazing, yourself."

He felt a frown bite into his brow. Had he verbalized the thought? Was he that discombobulated?

Something was wrong. He should set down the glass, push himself to a stand and make his apologies. He should hightail it out of there. Right now.

If he didn't, something was bound to happen. He knew it in his heart. Felt it in his gut and other places, too.

He had a sneaking suspicion it was the budding urges in those "other places" that kept him seated next to her on the sofa.

What astounded him was that he could be convinced about the right course of action and absolutely determined to follow it when he'd been out in the hallway, yet now he couldn't take action.

Things were different now, with her curvaceous body so close to his, her inviting scent filling his nostrils every time he inhaled. Her nearness was like some kind of mind-altering drug, or a couple of straight shots of tequila, blurring the line between right and wrong, slackening his determination to stick to his own personal promises to himself. In fact, he was now leaning more toward giving in to all those bad-boy compulsions that were taunting him, something he hadn't done in quite a while.

"And," she said silkily, "I'm not the only one who thinks so, either."

The thoughts crowding his head and the cravings that were stirring to life had made him lose track of the conversation, and Riley frowned.

Catherine chuckled and provided, "I'm not the only one who thinks you're amazing, silly." She squeezed his arm and pressed her forehead to his shoulder momentarily. Then she gazed up into his face and observed, "You're awfully preoccupied."

Her blue eyes flashed with a blatant boldness—an appealing bravado—that left him thinking she knew full well the sensuous turn his thoughts had taken.

He took a drink from his glass, barely tasting what he suspected must be very expensive wine.

"Anyway," she continued smoothly, "I met a couple of people today when I was leaving the clinic who had some nice things to say about you."

Yes, she knew he wanted her, and even though she was talking about a completely different topic, the lush awareness in her tone was sexy as hell.

So was the confidence tipping her chin, straightening her spine.

Riley fought to focus. "People?"

"Mm-hm."

Her little singsong response might have sounded like a

simple affirmative answer, but she was sending erotic messages. Messages his body was receiving, loud and clear.

She tipped up her wineglass and sipped. "Harry and Carol Higgins. They've been married for twenty-five years. I got talking to them about the clinic. They started coming when Dr. Richie was in charge. Harry said he was sure the clinic would fall apart when Dr. Richie disappeared, and he was pleasantly surprised that it hasn't. Carol said she knew it was all because of you. That you were fully devoted to making the clinic a success. And," she added, "they went on and on about a seminar you gave in which you encouraged people to continue to exercise and watch their diet, and assured everyone that losing weight was possible even without crutches."

He nodded. "That was the first week I was at the clinic. One of the things I noticed was how much emphasis everyone was putting on NoWait. It bothered me. I understand that, psychologically, it's easier for people to put faith and trust in something tangible, a prop, a crutch—in this case the oil—rather than to put faith and trust in themselves to conquer their problem. Whether that problem is weight, or tobacco addiction, or whatever, you have to find the strength within to unearth your solution."

"See there?" she said, leaning over and setting her glass down on the coffee table. "I've been trying to tell you that the knowledge you have really does help people."

As if it were the most natural thing in the world to do, she twisted her body and slid her bottom onto his lap. Riley's eyes widened. But he didn't protest.

She combed her fingers through his hair just above his ear.

An incredible sensation tumbled down the length of his spine and he fought off a shudder. Desire flared, and he grew rock-hard in the span of a single indrawn breath.

"Harry and Carol were optimistic and positive," she whispered. "And they gave a lot of the credit to you."

"That's nice." His murmured response was automatic. Unable to bend forward to set his glass on the coffee table with hers, he set it on the end table. Then he encircled both her forearms with his hands, pulled them to his chest. It was a knee-jerk defensive move, an attempt to slow things down so he'd have time to think. However, she didn't seem to take it that way at all.

She chose that moment to press forward. Doing so trapped her arms and his hands between them. Then she took his earlobe between her teeth.

He sucked air into his lungs and exhaled her name. The feel of her full breasts pressed against the backs of his hands made his brain haze over.

"Wait, wait," he murmured.

Catherine pulled away.

"What are you doing?" he asked.

The provocative smile she offered only fueled the hunger within him.

"I'm sitting on your lap."

"Y-yes," he stammered, "but—"

"And I'm giving your earlobe a taste. It's something I've wanted to do for a while now. And since I have to leave tomorrow night—"

"You're leaving?"

Her mouth pouted most seductively. "Yes, so you'd better prepare yourself because I couldn't possibly fly out of Portland before kissing you right here."

She traced the soft pad of her finger along the lower edge of his jaw, her touch as hot as a match flame.

Her head tilted, and her mouth was on him once again. Vaguely, he was aware of her hair brushing against his neck. Instinct alone forced him to tilt his head a fraction, to let her have her way. Her breasts were so close, so lush and firm, and he knew that all he had to do was shift the position of his hands and those ripe mounds would fill his palms.

"Catherine, Catherine." Once again he attempted to wrestle his way out of the passionate mire threatening to drown him.

She sat up, her fanny squirming dangerously against his steely length.

The clouds in her eyes couldn't have been described as anything other than pure, unadulterated lust. The magnitude of her passion seemed to deplete every single molecule of air from the room. He had difficulty breathing.

"You want this just as much as I do."

The certainty in her voice rocked him to the core. She was absolutely right. He did.

With no further thought, he released his hold on sanity.

Catherine's hands trembled as she gently cradled his face between her palms. Her blood raced through her body and her heart fluttered as swiftly as a hummingbird's wings. Although many thoughts jumbled in her head, every single one of them focused on one thing.

Riley.

Desire deepened his eyes to the color of rich, black coffee. The intensity of his stare made her go weak all over. Her limbs suddenly felt heavy, and time itself seemed to grow sluggish.

Ever so gently, she leaned forward and pressed her forehead to his. She closed her eyes and touched the tip of her nose to his cheek. He smelled good. Like warm cedar and some other woodsy scent.

A tiny shift allowed her to rub her cheek against his, the slight roughness of his five-o'clock shadow titillating the ever-growing craving inside her.

There was no doubt in her mind that he wanted her. She could sense his yearning throbbing on the thick air. She could see the hunger in his eyes. She could feel his rigid member pressing against her buttock. All that separated their naughty bits were mere swaths of thin fabric. His trousers. Her skirt.

The idea so excited her that her chest rose and fell with the quickening of her breath.

Unable to hold off any longer, Catherine kissed him. His lips were moist and fiery hot. When she parted her lips to deepen the kiss, her tongue was met with the faint sweet tang of wine.

The kiss they shared was deliciously long and lingering. There was a playfulness to their nibbling and tasting that paralleled the teasing and flirting relationship that they'd shared from the first.

His hands encircled her waist. With great purpose and forethought, she rotated her hips, grinding her rear against his lap. His groan delighted her.

She combed her fingers through his hair, reveling in the cool silkiness of it and marveling at how at odds it felt compared to the scorch of his kiss and the heat of his hands through the fabric of her blouse.

"Catherine." His tone grated against her mouth, filled with profound and heart-wrenching emotion.

Breathlessly, she went still. Her gaze locked with his, and the seconds that ticked by seemed to become protracted with a peculiar Alice-in-Wonderland distortion. Slowly she unfastened the buttons of her blouse, then, filled with a brash sauciness, she shrugged her shoulders and let the fabric fall from her body.

She reached around behind her and curled her fingers around his wrists. Their gazes never wavered as she guided her hands between them and then upward until he cupped her breasts in his palms.

Her exhalation was taut as a harp string, and she could almost hear the twang of desire resonating on it. Catherine arched her back, tipped up her chin and closed her eyes.

Riley dragged the pads of his thumbs across her nipples, and even through the lace of her bra, the sensation was enough to tighten them into hard nubs. Her breasts seemed to become heavy and swollen with need.

He rained kisses high on her chest, and then lower on the swell of each breast. He took one budded nipple into his mouth, wetting the lace of her bra with his tongue.

Riley suckled, and Catherine felt herself grow moist between her thighs.

She experienced a sudden and frantic urge to be free of her clothes, to feel his naked flesh against hers.

"Riley." Was that rusty voice coming from her throat? "Let's go to the bedroom."

Her attempt to scramble from his lap was clumsy at best, but the emotion zipping through her was frenetic and nearly more than she could bear.

He didn't immediately move. "Are you sure?"

Words wouldn't come, so she simply pleaded, "Riley!"

He shoved his way off the couch and took her in his arms. His kiss was rougher now and just what Catherine needed to satisfy the yearning that was quickly driving her to the very brink.

Without breaking their flurry of impassioned kisses, they made their way around the obstacle course of sofa, tables and chairs. She loosened his tie and tugged it over his head, then tossed it aside. He pulled her to him tightly, long enough to reach around and unzip her skirt. She gave her hips a little shimmy and the skirt fell to the floor.

She kicked off her shoes, and he slid out of his loafers. The buttons of his shirt gave her a bit of trouble, and after communicating her frustration in the form of a small groan, he unfastened them for her. Then she tugged the shirt off his wide shoulders and flung it carelessly.

In the hallway, Catherine reached for his belt buckle. The metal felt warm against her skin as she loosened it. A single button and a quick zip relieved him of his dress pants. The trousers pooled at his feet and he stepped out of them just as they reached the doorway of her bedroom. He bent and flicked off one sock, then the other.

He was bare except for his burgundy boxers.

"Oooo, sexy." She grinned. "And you have sexy legs, too. And sexy feet."

His voice was gravelly as he commented, "No one's ever told me that my feet are sexy."

He darted at her, swooping her into his arms, and she squealed with both surprise and glee.

A few short steps brought them to the bed, where he unceremoniously dumped her. She bounced on the mattress, laughing. He sank onto the bed beside her.

It seemed his hands were everywhere at once, sliding down the length of her neck, over her arms and breasts, stilling for a scant second on her hips. His palm came to rest on her flat tummy, and when he looked into her eyes, all humor was gone. The need expressed in his dark gaze seemed illimitable, and in an instant the bouncy, lively air that had flashed between them dissolved so suddenly it was as if it had never existed.

His mouth crushed against hers at the same time that

his fingers inched farther down her body. The elastic of her silk lace bikini panties presented no hindrance to his erotic exploration, and she quivered when he maneuvered his way beneath them.

She gasped when he combed through her sensitive curls.

He kissed her cheek and her jaw, and when he reached that most mysterious part of her, he lifted his head to look at her.

"You're wet," he groaned softly.

Slipping his fingers a fraction lower, he entered her, and it was Catherine's turn to moan.

Riley ravished her breasts with his lips and his tongue, and all the while the expert ministrations of his fingers down below carried her closer and closer to some unfamiliar place. Gladly—no, eagerly—she rode the incredible, wonderful and most foreign wave of ecstasy.

The surge of emotions he created inside her swelled higher, and Catherine whimpered. She nipped at the corded curve of his neck, slid her hands over his muscular back, kissed the hardness of his smooth shoulder.

Suddenly, sensation rushed at her with the power of a tsunami, lifting, spinning, tossing her as it curled in on itself and crashed at what felt like the very core of her being.

She cried his name, panting as if she'd run a great distance. Her eyes wide open now, she saw that he was looking down into her face as she gasped and smiled in pure ecstasy.

Catherine realized that she'd become so focused on her own pleasure that she'd completely forgotten about his.

"I'm sorry," she murmured.

"Don't you dare apologize."

His expression articulated such unspoken tenderness that her heart ached from the sight of it.

Riley unfastened her bra, and then curling his fingers beneath the lace of her panties, he tugged them down her legs and over her feet. He pulled off his boxers and then slid on top of her.

The weight of him felt good, felt right, and Catherine sighed contentedly. His chest was hard beneath her palms, the springy hairs tickling her skin.

He nuzzled her neck, and hunger sparked to life inside her all over again. But this need felt different. Condensed and intense. Oddly deeper. Harder to reach.

She didn't quite understand what was happening to her body, the feelings tormenting her. All she knew was that she needed more. Much more.

Riley kissed her face and shoulders, the swell of her breasts, shifting his hips just enough to get her to part her legs for him. For a moment, his steely rod pressed against her stomach and she trembled deliciously.

Then he nestled himself into the most natural and most wonderful position that Mother Nature had invented. His elbows supported most of his weight, but his hips pressed against her hips, and Catherine felt overwhelmed with that luscious breathlessness again.

Longing wholly consumed him, too, and she couldn't believe the joy that brought her.

Instinctively, she tilted her hips up a fraction, and he slid into her with one powerful stroke. Pain shot through her body and she grimaced.

"Catherine?"

Doubt edged his tone, and before the pain could fully subside, she felt a fluttering panic threaten the wondrous moment.

"I want this, Riley," she whispered. She reached up and skimmed his jaw with her fingers. "I want you."

Her touch had him closing his eyes. His second thrust was gentle, and it only brought a twinge of discomfort. Pleasure relaxed Riley's features, and Catherine got caught up in just watching him. She realized why he'd refused her apology before, because he, too, had become enthralled by the show.

Soon, though, passion sprouted and expanded like a swiftly growing vine, spiraling, twisting, curling in every nook and cranny until she was once again filled to the brim with lush, heart-pounding passion.

Feeling feverish and elated beyond her wildest imaginings, Catherine let Riley sweep her away.

Nine

Carrie Martin fought back her bitter disappointment. She'd scoured every pool hall in Portland, showing Richard's picture to anyone who would listen to her. And her inquiries seemed to grow more frantic after each failure.

She'd been ready to give up when it hit her: If he didn't want to be found, he would very likely steer clear of Portland. The thought had excited her and fired up her determination to find him. So she'd called the restaurant and asked her boss to find a replacement for her. When he'd assumed she'd caught the bug that was going around and told her he hoped she felt better soon, Carrie didn't set him straight, realizing she wouldn't be able to rest until she found her ex-husband.

Country Cove Pool Hall was located in a strip mall. The parking lot was small, and only a few of the spaces were occupied. She'd probably strike out here, as well, but she needed to check, just for her own peace of mind.

During her hunt, she'd been in many different establishments. All of them, it seemed, had their own unique ambiance. Just as her son had feared, she'd been in bars, both cruddy and classy, that had pool rooms. She'd also been to numerous billiard halls, businesses that catered to the serious pool player. Then there were the so-called family gaming centers, catering to G-rated entertainment and offering electronic arcade games as well as a variety of other amusements. Country Cove was such a family place.

Clean and smoke-free, the room was large and well-lit. Upbeat pop music filtered through the sound system. A bored-looking teen sat behind the counter near the door. Carrie saw a father and son engaged in some sort of fantasy battle game, both wearing large black goggles and swinging futuristic sabers in the air as they fought off some unseen enemy.

"Pool tables?" Carrie asked the young man near the cash register.

He gave a vague point and went back to reading his comic book.

Carrie trudged toward the back and saw the neon sign flashing Billiards.

Richard was the only person in the pool room. The sight of him filled Carrie with a huge sense of relief, but following swiftly on its heels was an immense foreboding. What on earth would she say? How could she possibly explain?

She'd gone over all that a hundred times, but now that Richard was right in front of her, her mind drew a blank.

He concentrated on a shot. The stick hit the cue ball with a sharp crack and pool balls scattered across the green felt surface of the table. Stepping back to assess his next move, Richard studied the balls. Carrie shifted, and his gaze shot to the doorway.

Overwhelming emotion filled his face. Clearly, he felt cornered. He gave the emergency exit a darting glance.

"Richard," Carrie said, "we need to talk."

His jaw tensed and something simmered in his dark eyes. Resentment? Ire?

"You have every right to be angry with me. Please, let's sit down and talk. Let me explain. This has been too long in coming."

The pool stick slid from his hand, the butt coming to rest on the tile floor. Surprisingly, he relented with a nod. "Far too long," he agreed.

Just minutes later, they sat at one of the round plastic tables outside Country Cove, nursing sodas that they'd purchased from a nearby vending machine, not because either of them was thirsty, but because they both needed some semblance of normalcy in this most abnormal situation.

The first thing Richard had done was to comment on how different she looked. He still had trouble believing he'd met and talked with her at the clinic without recognizing her. The awe and admiration in both his tone and his expression made Carrie beam with pride, but then awkwardness settled over them, unsettling them both.

Carrie simply cut loose and allowed everything that was in her heart to spill out. She rolled her life into a nutshell for him because she wanted him to know everything. Everything, that was, except the information about their son. As Jason's mother, she felt it was her job to protect him, at all costs. She wanted to feel Richard out first. She needed to be fairly certain that he'd be receptive to the idea that he was a father before she revealed that fact.

"So," she said, summing up her story, "I've been beside myself, teetering between feeling happy that I'd found you after so many years, and angry about feelings that can only be described as abandonment. And that's why I exploded that day in the clinic. I should never have said those things in front of all those people. I should never have—"

"Carrie." Richard's hand slid over hers, and she went silent. "Stop feeling bad about that. My life was out of control long before you showed up. Things were bound to catch up with me sooner or later."

He looked so wounded, and Carrie's heart went out to him.

"What things?" she asked. "What are you talking about?"

His gaze slid away and he pulled his hand from hers. He was quiet for an uncomfortably long time. Sensing she shouldn't push him, Carrie remained patient.

Finally Richard shook his head, unable to look her in the eye. "That day at the clinic when you laid everything out on the line like you did—"

He stopped at her bark of acidic laughter. "Is that what you're choosing to call it? I refer to it as my 'awful scene,' my 'temper tantrum' and 'the day I made a royal ass of myself.'"

Richard ignored her. "You just shot from the hip."

"I shot from the hip, the shoulder, the foot, the head." Her mouth twisted in irritation at her own behavior. "I feel as if I thoroughly annihilated you."

He caught her eye then, his gaze softening. This was the old Richard she knew. The man she had married and then lost so many years ago.

"That's a little harsh," he said. "I'm right here, alive and kicking. Quit being so hard on yourself." He toyed with the soda can in front of him. "The truth is you did me a great favor, Carrie."

How that could be, she had no idea.

"After I left Florida," he told her, "something happened to me. I'd always been ambitious, you know that. And I allowed that ambition to ruin the best thing in my life."

An unexpected delight rolled through Carrie like an electric charge. Of all the things she'd expected to come out of this discussion, that had not been one of them.

"I'm glad you remarried," he continued. "I'm glad you found some happiness. You deserve it, Carrie."

The Healthy Living Clinic clients who were so down on Richard were wrong. She'd been wrong. He really could be kind and caring.

"I, on the other hand," he told her, "haven't been so lucky."

She didn't like the black cloud that suddenly engulfed him.

"What are you talking about?" she teased, attempting to keep her voice light. "You've made a great success of yourself." Although she cringed inside, she added, "Dr. Richie."

His jaw clenched. "Oh, how I hate that name."

His response shocked her. "But I thought— Isn't what you wanted? What you'd worked for?"

He sighed in disgust. "Only because of Browell."

"Dr. Terry?" This only confused her more.

Richard's voice turned both bitter and childish. "'Live Airy with Dr. Terry.' That man loves to tell people about their weight problems, yet he's a redheaded cow. And he's all high and mighty about domestic troubles, but I'll bet if we did a little snooping we'd find out he's had three wives."

Carrie couldn't believe what she was hearing. "Richard, why would you be jealous of Terry Browell?"

"He's in every magazine you pick up."

"I've seen you in the newspapers, and in magazines, too."

"I've had a small piece in *Pacific Northwest* magazine. He was on the cover of *Time,* Carrie. Everywhere you look it's 'Dr. Terry, this,' or 'Dr. Terry, that.' My success is very much regional. Dr. Eats-to-be-Merry has gone *national.* Millions tune into his show every day."

"But I saw you on TV," she said, hearing the slight accusation in her tone. "That's how I found you."

"Those were advertisements. I had to come up with funding for those. To promote my seminars. A huge difference." He slugged back a drink from his can. "When people at the clinic started calling me Dr. Richie, I let them even though I couldn't stand the sound of it. I'd worked so hard to come up with a good, sturdy name. Dr. Strong is what I wanted to be called, and here people were referring to me as Richie. It makes me feel four years old. But I knew they were comparing me to Browell, so I let it slide. Now I'm sorry I ever did."

"I think," Carrie observed quietly, "that you're the one who's being too hard on himself. You've done some good work at the clinic. You've helped people. And that was your goal from the very beginning. I remember."

Confidence allowed her to speak the final two words firmly.

"I did have good intentions. I really did, Carrie." He shrugged. "I still do. But I've made an awful lot of mistakes. In my professional life and in my personal life. I've had a lot of affairs, Carrie. And I...haven't treated the women very well. I'm ashamed to admit it, but I've broken more than a few hearts."

She wasn't sure how to respond. The nurturer in her spoke up when she murmured, "Well, you can't fix a problem until you know one exists. You've recognized something in you that needs to be put right. You can do it, Richard. I know you can. You're a smart man."

Now it was his turn to snicker derisively. "Oh, yeah, I'm smart, all right. Smart enough to invent an oil meant to help people lose weight, but not quite clever—or patient—enough to perform some simple tests before handing it out to dozens of people." His dark gaze clouded with trouble.

Carrie told him, "They've stopped using it. They've collected as much as they could."

"I guess that's for the best."

"Dr. Jacobs wants you to come back to the clinic, Richard."

"I'm sure he does. Handing over my head on a silver platter will look great on his résumé."

"No," she told him, "you don't understand. The hospital is planning tests for NoWait. They want you to oversee the lab work."

"I don't understand. My oil was making everyone act very peculiarly."

Peculiar was a mild word to describe how that oil had people behaving. "They're testing the oil for exactly that reason. If it turns out that NoWait can help people who suffer from sexual…difficulties, then Dr. Jacobs seems to think it could put Portland General on the map. What he told me was that there could be lots of money to be made." She slid her fingers down the damp exterior of her soda can. "And if NoWait has the potential to make Portland General famous…"

His eyebrows arched. "It can make *me* famous. It's *my* oil. I invented it."

"Yes, but Rich, please go slow. Let them do all the testing they want. You don't want any more mistakes."

He nodded. "You're right. You're absolutely right. I'm finished with mistakes. I'm going to dot every *i* and cross every *t* from here on out. I'll go see Dr. Jacobs first thing in the morning."

The gratitude in Richard's dark gaze made her heart melt right down her ribcage.

"Thanks, Carrie, for hunting me down."

She nodded, then she was attacked with a sudden case of nerves. Now was the time. She needed to tell him.

"I—I, uh," she stammered, "I had another reason for finding you, Richard."

"Another reason?"

"Yes, I really wanted to apologize for my behavior at the clinic," she said, hedging for time. "And I wanted to pass on the message from Dr. Jacobs. But there's something else, too. Something you should have been told long ago."

He just sat there waiting.

"There was another reason I looked for you after we separated," she said.

"But you said you looked for me because you had a change of heart."

The tone of his voice told her he was hoping she wasn't refuting that fact.

"And I did," she assured him. "Have a change of heart about our breakup, I mean. But there was another reason, as well."

Her heart hammered a mile a minute and blood whooshed through her ears. Oh, Lord, was she going to be able to do this without passing out?

"Carrie? Are you all right?"

She nodded. "Give me a second."

Jason crept into her thoughts. God, how she loved her son. He was the image of Richard. That boy was what had kept her going after her marriage had failed. Jason had been the reason she'd taken that second chance at love…with gratifying results. She and Ralph had enjoyed many happy years together.

However, she'd always wondered what kind of father Richard would have been. And she'd dreamed of this moment forever, it seemed.

Now it was here.

"Richard," she said with as much calmness as she could muster, "you're a father. We have a son."

A soft thump in the dark woke Catherine from a deep sleep. She felt trapped by the tangle of sheets, momentarily confused by her nakedness.

In an instant, though, it all came flooding back. Riley, and his kisses, and the extraordinary love they'd made right here on this very bed.

She stretched out languidly, every part of her, mind, body and soul, feeling heavy and fluid with complete satiation.

Like a fairy-tale knight in shining armor who had stepped into real life, Riley had swooped her into his arms in true romantic fashion and had carried her to the bed. The memory was heartrendingly sweet, one that Catherine could hold tight to for all time.

The two of them had become so caught up in the frenzy of passion that neither of them had given dinner a second thought. She'd have to toss out the Chinese take-out she'd left sitting on the counter.

Another soft sound in the dark made her lift her head. "Riley?" she said softly.

"Sorry. Didn't mean to wake you."

"What are you doing?" She glanced at the clock. "It's four-thirty in the morning. Come back to bed."

Speaking those four small words was like flipping on a switch. Catherine felt embers glowing to life deep in her belly.

"I can't. I need to go. I just have to find my boxers. I've gathered the rest of my things in the living room."

"Flip on the light. It's okay."

"I don't need the light, Catherine. I'm fine." She heard him sliding into his underwear. "I'll call you later."

A shaft of dim light widened across the floor when he opened the bedroom door. Riley's form blocked the light for a mere nanosecond. If Catherine had blinked she'd have missed it. Then he closed the door behind him.

Great, she thought. He was so overwhelmed by what had happened between them that he hadn't even thought to kiss her goodbye.

Catherine chuckled as she flopped back against the down pillow. That was what she wanted in a man, in a husband. Someone who was overwhelmed by her.

The contentment making her feel light as air quickly became muddied as the thought of a husband and marriage reminded her of the ever-ticking clock, of the alarm that was about to jangle and send her flying home to Lextanya.

It had been that crushing pressure that had provoked Catherine into taking what she'd seen as the static situation between her and Riley firmly in hand and forcing something to happen. And even though she might not be all that proud of her method, the result had been more than she could have ever hoped for.

Still, now that Riley was gone and she was all alone

with her pleasure cooling, Catherine began to feel guilty over having manipulated him with that oil.

Getting a vial of the NoWait had been easy enough. Once she'd decided to actually take a bottle—*stealing* was such a nasty little word—all she'd had to do was slip through the door marked Employees Only. Once in the hallway, she'd noticed that the whole atmosphere had changed.

The public part of the clinic was decorated in calm shades of blues and pearly greens, but the walls and floor of this hall had been stark white. She'd hit the jackpot in the very first door she'd entered. Complicated scientific equipment filled the black marble counters around the perimeter of the pristine lab. On the long, narrow island in the center of the room, Catherine had found a small stack of manila file folders marked NoWait. To the left of the door sat racks of small blue vials.

She hadn't touched a thing in the room—except for the one vial she'd plucked from the rack and slipped into her purse. Her heart had been beating hard and strong even though she hadn't seen a soul coming or going. However, a heavy guilt had moved in alongside that tiny bottle of oil.

Pure stubborn determination—and that ever-present ticking clock—had spurred her forward, though, without too much problem.

She'd left a note for Riley with the receptionist, and then she'd hopped into a taxi that had taken her to the Boys and Girls Club where she tried to fill up the long afternoon.

After picking up containers of Chinese food, she'd come back to the hotel to get herself ready for Riley's arrival. She'd showered and dressed and put on a bit of makeup. Then she'd pulled out the NoWait.

The only information she'd had was that the oil was a

topical treatment. But she had no idea just how much she was supposed to use.

I only used a little.

The trainer's assertion to Faye had echoed through Catherine's head. But how much was a little? A small spot? A quarter ounce? Half an ounce? More?

Catherine had dabbed some behind her ears and on her wrists. But then she worried that she hadn't used enough so she'd smoothed some between her breasts and on the backs of her knees, and just for good measure, she'd splashed a bit behind each ankle.

Remembering the passion that had seemed to hypnotize Riley, she wondered if maybe she had gone a little overboard with the NoWait.

Catherine heard the front door close as Riley left, and she slid down under the sheet, the cool cotton caressing her body as she vividly recalled his hot kisses, his tender touch. They had made love for what had seemed like hours before falling asleep, exhausted, in each other's arms. It had been the absolute best, most wonderful and memorable night of her life. And she refused to regret any of it.

She didn't care if she had used too much.

Her time with Riley had been well worth it.

Although the meeting was being held in his office, Riley didn't even try to pretend he was in charge. Portland General Hospital director, Dr. David Graham, had been strutting back and forth across the room like the rooster who owned the henhouse since he'd arrived.

When Riley had entered the clinic this morning, Dr. Richard Strong had been waiting for him. Furious beyond measure with himself for succumbing to his weaknesses last night, Riley knew it wasn't really the best time to be dealing with the whole NoWait situation. However, these days nothing seemed to happen the way Riley expected, so what the hell did it matter that Dr. Strong had shown up today of all days?

There had been a few awkward moments between the two men, naturally, since Riley had taken Dr. Richie's position when he'd disappeared nearly a month ago. However, Riley had put the man at ease quickly enough. Richard Strong may have made a mistake or two—or even three—over the course of his career, and stories about him abounded at the clinic. Yet Riley liked to form his own opinions about people. What he swiftly learned this morning was that Richard was charismatic and intelligent and daring. He was a person willing to take a chance in order to make his ideas come to fruition. Risks always came with a multitude of possibilities, good and bad, so Riley decided Richard was entitled to some missteps through the years.

They chatted awhile about the clinic in general. And after assuaging Richard's fears and assuring him that he was indeed needed in the lab, Riley had called Faye and Dr. Graham and asked them to come to his office. Riley knew Faye would need to know of Richard's return, and that the hospital director would appreciate the opportunity to give Richard the official welcome back.

And that was just what Dr. Graham had been doing for the past ten minutes. He buttered up Dr. Richie to the point that Riley feared the man would slide right out of his chair.

"Now that you're back," David Graham said to Richard, "we can finally get moving with the testing."

"I'm looking forward to it." Richard shifted in his seat. "Can you tell me where we're at in the lab?"

David looked at Riley expectantly.

"I've read over the protocol for the experiments," Riley

told them both. "But I don't have much experience with laboratory research. Dr. Lassen's been keeping an eye on things. She's hired a study director, a chemist and two lab techs."

Excitement brightened Richard's expression.

"She'll be able to fill you in when she arrives." Riley glanced toward his office door. "I wonder where she is? I called her—"

"Oh, I caught Faye out in the hall before I came in," Dr. Graham said. "I sent her for some fresh coffee. I thought Dr. Richie might enjoy some before he gets to work."

A flash of irritation shot through Riley, and he clenched his jaw in an attempt to keep it in check.

"You want me to start today?" Pleasant surprise perked up Dr. Richie's tone.

"I sure do." David nodded enthusiastically. "I think all that nasty hoo-ha that happened last month has pretty much died down. Don't you, Dr. Jacobs? In fact, I think after a month or so we might be able to talk about your returning to your original post running things here at the clinic. In fact, maybe a promotion to Chief of Staff might be in order."

Riley was shocked. And as he sat there listening to Dr. Graham wax on, his hackles rose.

"If work in the lab goes well," Richard commented, "I was hoping this might springboard into something even bigger."

Dr. Graham's grin was accompanied by more animated nodding. "I hope you're right. I hope this turns into something big for all of us."

"If I may make a request?" Richard asked.

"Of course." Dr. Graham looked expectant.

Richard Strong planted both feet on the floor. "I'd like

to run a seminar. It's something I've been thinking about while I was…away from the clinic. It's called Losing Weight Through Cognition: the ability to combine knowledge with reasoning, awareness and intuition."

"I love the idea!" Graham barked out. "It'll give the clients a chance to get reacquainted with you. And—"

"Excuse me," Riley cut in. "I'm sorry to burst your bubble. But I think the staff here at the clinic will have to get together and decide if a new seminar should be offered. The staff know the clients very well. They know the atmosphere. They're much more qualified to project the success of a workshop given by Dr. Strong."

"I understand." Richard smoothed his palms together. "And I agree. You talk to the staff, Dr. Jacobs, and let me know."

"Actually," Riley decided to insert, "Dr. Lassen is in charge of staff meetings and the seminar schedule. Correct me if I'm wrong, Dr. Strong, but that's the way things were when you were here before, wasn't it?"

Annoyance etched David Graham's face.

Just then Faye Lassen let herself into the office carrying a tray laden with four cups. The smell of coffee immediately permeated the air.

"Hello, everyone," Faye greeted. "I brought coffee—"

"I've got to be going," Dr. Graham interrupted. "But I'd appreciate it, Faye, if you'd fill Dr. Richie in on everything that's happening in the lab."

"Well, I've got a lot on my plate this morning, sir," Faye said.

"I'm sure you can work things out," the hospital director insisted.

Ire had Riley blurting, "I'll cover for you, Faye. I'm free most of the morning."

Dr. Graham was busy pumping Dr. Richie's hand. "Glad to have you back." Over his shoulder, he said, "Dr. Jacobs, Faye, keep up the good work." With that Portland General's director breezed out the door.

Anger rolled through Riley. "Excuse me for a moment."

"No problem," Richard told him. "Dr. Lassen and I have a lot to talk about."

Out in the hall, Riley jogged several steps to catch up with David Graham.

The elderly man looked surprised to see him.

"You're not seriously considering reinstating Richard Strong as director of the clinic, are you?"

"Don't worry." The man didn't slow his steps. "We'll find a nice cushy spot for you—"

"I'm not worried about me," Riley snapped. "I'm worried about the clinic. That man can't be trusted. He walked out a month ago without looking back, and he didn't bother contacting anyone."

"He deserves a second chance. You should know something about second chances."

Riley smoldered.

"Besides, we opened this clinic on Dr. Richie's good reputation." Dr. Graham shoved open the heavy glass door. Riley pushed open its twin. And they stepped out into the morning sunshine. "We can afford to overlook his small indiscretion. I'm surprised that you can't see what a benefit he could be to the clinic."

Riley didn't comment right away, only continued to walk toward the hospital. Then he said, "Dr. Strong is obviously on to something." What, exactly, could be anyone's guess. "It's clear that NoWait does affect people. He should be involved in the testing. But he isn't qualified to run the clinic."

David Graham stopped short. "What are you saying? Don't tell me that you're looking to stay on because—"

"My post here is temporary," he said pointedly. "You yourself promised me that when you sent me over here. What I'm saying is that you're overlooking the one person who is qualified and who truly deserves the job."

He blinked, clearly baffled. "And who would that be?"

"The fact that you honestly don't know really ticks me off."

"Careful, Dr. Jacobs."

Riley inhaled deeply, mentally counting to ten in order to calm down. Finally, he said, "For your information, Dr. Lassen is the person you should ask to take over at the clinic."

"Faye?" he blustered.

"Dr. Lassen has earned her medical degree. She has earned the right to be called doctor. She deserves your respect. You're making a grave error in judgment by refusing to see that. You're also making a grave error in sending her after your lunch and sending her for coffee that you don't even have the decency to drink."

"Faye doesn't mind."

"She's not going to allow you to think she minds because of who you are, but I can guarantee you she minds. However, I think you're well aware of that."

A muscle near Graham's eye twitched, but he remained silent.

Riley continued, "I suspect that Dr. Lassen has been running the clinic from the beginning. I think it's time she's given the title to go along with the work she's already doing."

"What you need to understand is that Dr. Lassen is married. Soon she'll be having babies and she'll retire to raise her family."

"That's blatant discrimination! Do you have any idea what an attorney—were she to hire one—could do with a statement like that?"

"I—"

"Besides that," Riley barreled ahead, "I think you should know that Dr. Lassen's dedication to this clinic has caused her and her husband to separate."

Graham just glared.

"That woman has given her all to the success of this place. You need to realize that. If anyone ever deserved to be Chief of Staff at that clinic, it's she."

"I think you've said enough, Jacobs. Faye will never make Chief as long as I'm director of this hospital. She's a woman. And in the future, you'd better watch how you talk to me. I could have your ass in a sling. You know I have the means." His bushy brows drew together. "We both know what *you* are. A common criminal."

Riley raked agitated fingers through his hair as he watched the old man stomp away. The anger pumping through him was hot as a blaze.

"Hey, there! You're looking particularly sexy and satiated this morning."

He turned to see Catherine coming toward him. Sunlight glinted golden off her flaxen hair. Her smile and her blue eyes flashed alluringly. But neither the sight of her lovely face nor the teasing in her tone was enough to snuff out his fury.

Riley glowered at her. "Why the hell didn't you tell me you were a virgin?"

Ten

The magnitude of Riley's anger hit Catherine full force. Her smile disappeared without a trace. Self-consciously, she glanced around at the people coming and going on the sidewalk.

Finding her tongue, she quietly asked, "Do we have to talk about this out here?"

Without a word, Riley stalked toward the entrance of the clinic.

Refusing to be intimidated by him, she said, "I'm surprised that you're angry. Everything seemed fine when you left this morning."

"I'm surprised that you're surprised."

They rounded a corner in the hall and came face to face with Faye, who was with a man Catherine had never seen here at the clinic.

"Catherine, hi," Faye greeted. "How are you doing today?"

All those years of etiquette training kicked in and Catherine returned Faye's smile. "I'm well, thanks. Yourself?"

"Just fine. This is Dr. Richie," she introduced. "Doctor, this is Catherine Houston. She's been coming to the clinic for about two weeks now."

Catherine could feel Riley brooding beside her.

"Dr. Richie." Catherine offered her hand. "How nice to finally meet you. You've been the talk of this place since I first arrived."

The man's dark eyes grew hooded. "I'll bet."

Faye turned her attention to Riley. "I'm taking Dr. Richie into the lab. I'll send someone to clear up the coffee mess I left in your office."

"There's no need for that. I can do it myself." Riley's tone was curt enough to make Faye pause.

"You okay?" she asked him.

"I'm fine." The words were snipped tight enough so that no further discussion would dare be required.

Faye looked from Riley to Catherine, unasked questions clouding her eyes. Catherine shot her a look of warning. Then Faye leveled her gaze on Riley.

"I left my schedule on your desk," she told him. "You still up to covering for me today?"

"I said I would, and I will."

"Okay, then." But she clearly sounded unconvinced.

"Nice to have met you, Dr. Richie," Catherine rushed to say before hurrying to catch Riley who had started toward his office.

She barely made it through the door when he slammed it behind her, the thump making her start.

"Okay," he practically growled at her, "I'm ready for an

explanation. Why would a woman who has saved herself for as long as you have—"

"Just stop right there! You're talking like I'm a wrinkled old prune of a spinster or something. I'll have you know—"

"Do not change the subject, Catherine. Don't go off on a tirade. You know exactly what I'm trying to say."

"My virginity is mine to give to whomever I please," she said. "I should think you'd be happy that you were my first. Correct me if I have the wrong idea, but it's pretty well known that you American men love to put those notches on your bedposts."

"Who's being insulting now, Catherine?" he charged. "I resent being lumped into a stupid stereotype with every other American man. And I also resent your insinuation that I make it a practice to engage in meaningless sex for the sole purpose of notching my bedpost." His tone turned gruff as he added, "My bed doesn't even have posts, thank you very much."

"I'd say you're the one on a tirade," she muttered. Then she tipped her head a fraction. "So are you saying that last night meant something to you?"

From the look on his handsome face, she could tell she'd turned the tables on him. She could also tell that he didn't like it one bit.

"There you go again," he said. "Changing the subject."

She tipped up her chin, arching her eyebrows. "Well, you can't expect me to answer your questions if you're unwilling to answer mine."

He countered pointedly, "But you haven't answered my question. And I asked mine first."

That was true enough; however, panic set in and Catherine wasn't even sure how to respond without exposing details of her life she wasn't ready to reveal. So instead, she accused, "You wanted me last night just as much as I wanted you."

"Of course I wanted you! I'm a red-blooded male. You're a beautiful woman, Catherine. On the inside as well as on the outside. What man wouldn't want you?"

Catherine's arms fell to her sides. The sigh that soughed through her when she heard those words could only be described as pure gratification, airy, light and heart-lifting.

"I fought the attraction I felt for you," he continued, "from the very first time we met."

"I knew it! But *why?*" she cried, unable to quell the plaintive quality in those two small words.

He paused, his expression turning guarded. "For lots of reasons." He moistened his lips. "You made it clear you would only be in Portland for a while, and you said you were only looking for a friend."

But his gaze slid from hers.

"Oh, come on. I've been doing all I can to entice you into—"

"But at the restaurant, you said—"

"There's no way you didn't know I wanted things to progress!" she accused. "I've been flirting with— *We've* been flirting with *each other* from the start. Come on. Admit it."

He didn't speak right away, so she pushed, "Why, Riley? Why would you not want to act on what you were feeling?" Her chuckle was low. "Once you did, you sure got a reaction out of me."

"You don't have to remind me," he said with a scowl. "I was there last night. Your reaction is forever seared into my brain."

Catherine suppressed the delighted grin threatening to

curl her lips. "So..." She lifted her hands palms up. "Why'd you fight it so hard?"

What she really wanted to ask was why he'd forced her to use the NoWait. But she didn't dare. She was desperate to hear all about how he'd truly wanted to take her to bed *before* she'd used the oil that had aroused their sexual desires to the point that neither of them could possibly resist.

Riley sighed, and for several seconds she feared he didn't intend to explain.

He crossed his arms over his chest. "I knew about you right from the start," he began.

He knew? The question pierced her brain like an arrow the same time it shot from her mouth. "You knew?"

What did he know? That she'd lied about her name? That she was of royal birth?

"You see," he continued, evidently not realizing her distress, "I dated a girl once who came from a well-to-do family."

Catherine relaxed.

"I've already told you that I'm from the blue-collar world, Catherine. Needless to say, the girl's father wouldn't accept me as suitable. I was utterly humiliated and I vowed that I wouldn't suffer that kind of embarrassment again. And the only way to do that would be to steer clear of women like you. Women who exist in a whole different realm than the one I exist in."

If he only knew how perfect his word choices were.

Although his story was a tad skimpy on the details, she still felt great empathy for him and his experience.

"I'm sorry, Riley," she said. "Every person deserves to be treated with respect and dignity, no matter what their financial situation might be."

"You've been so closemouthed about your family," he said, "and where you're from. It probably wasn't fair of me to take for granted how I might or might not be accepted. But my past experience was so hellish that I never really allowed myself to think about it much, anyway. I never want to encounter anything like that again, Catherine. Ever."

Guilt, thick and choking, gathered in her chest, rose to her throat. How would she ever tell him the full truth about herself? He thought she came merely from a wealthy family. And he'd been hurt by people like that; he'd been judged and humiliated by them. Keeping secrets from him about her identity had been wrong. The idea had seemed so harmless when she'd made the decision to do it, but now she was learning that her secret wasn't at all harmless.

She swallowed, but remained silent.

Riley lifted his gaze to her face, his dark eyes intense. "Okay," he said quietly, "I've answered your questions. I've told you why I tried not to get too involved with you. Now it's time for you to answer mine."

Dread chilled her blood and she nearly shivered. She didn't want to face the truth. And she sure didn't want Riley to know it.

"Why, Catherine?" His coffee-colored eyes bored into her. "Why didn't you tell me you were a virgin? Why did you let me—"

He stopped, obviously upset by the questions he was asking.

When she remained quiet, he gently demanded, "Why would you give me such a precious gift?"

The realities of her life closed in on her, and thoughts whirled in her head. Her knees felt weak and she felt the urgent need to sit down.

She went to one of the high-backed leather chairs and sat, balling her hands into fists and settling them onto her lap.

"Catherine?"

Running from home had seemed so easy. But there was no running from this. Riley wasn't going to allow her to escape.

"I—I needed t-to know," she stammered, her insides quaking. "I wanted to be wanted. For me."

Her answer only confused him. His frown told her that.

She tried again. "I wanted to be a normal, regular woman who was desired by a normal, regular man. I—I couldn't bear the idea of living the rest of my life with…" She let the rest of the sentence trail off and she looked down, suddenly surprised by how white her knuckles had become.

She tried to relax.

This was Riley. She'd gone out with him. Talked with him. Teased him. They'd spent lots of time together over the past weeks. They'd become friends before they were lovers. Surely he wouldn't judge her. He wasn't that kind of person.

"I'm expected to marry when I go home, Riley." The calmness in her tone astounded her. "I barely know the man. But I do know I'll never love him. He's only agreed to marry me because of who I am. I could never respect a man who would do such a thing. And I could never love a man I don't respect." A lump rose in her throat and moisture scalded the backs of her eyelids. "I didn't consciously set out to sleep with you, Riley. I'd just thought I might have a little naughty fun." The words sounded so immature when she said them. "But I'm glad it happened. I'm glad you and I slept together. I can't abide the idea of having to give my…of having to lose my—" She inhaled a shaky breath. Her voice was small as she said, "I'm glad my first time won't be in those circumstances, Riley. It's going to be bad enough sleeping with—"

With a man who, she knew in her heart, wouldn't be faithful. Who cared nothing at all for her as a person. Who had only offered to marry her for the prestige and advantage that came with her name and title and wealth.

It was all so cold and unfeeling. No wonder normal, everyday people had preconceived notions about the nobility of the world. They were a quirky bunch.

She realized suddenly that Riley hadn't said a word. Catherine looked up at him and saw that his face had gone quite pale.

He lowered himself into the chair flanking hers and stared off across the room. They were silent for some time.

Finally Riley asked, "Who are you exactly, Catherine?"

She squared her shoulders. He knew much of her secret. He might as well learn everything. "My name is Catherine von Husden."

A tiny line bit into the space between his dark eyebrows. "I read about a von Husden in the papers. He visited Portland not too long ago." He shook his head. "He married a local woman and then returned to his home to be crowned king."

"That would be Max, my cousin. King of Lantanya."

"Lantanya?"

"An island kingdom in the Adriatic Sea," she explained. "Just off the coasts of Albania and Italy."

He nodded vaguely, but she could tell the information she was relaying was overwhelming him.

"Your English is excellent," he said. "But you do have a Mediterranean accent."

He was attempting to conduct himself as if what he was hearing was the most normal thing in the world.

"I had an American nanny for years." Catherine crossed her legs and nervously smoothed the fabric of her skirt. "My sister did, as well. My father thought it was important for us to master the English language."

"Do you speak other languages? I remember at dinner you rattled off the names of those wines so easily."

His tone had taken on a foggy quality that Catherine did her best to ignore. His subconscious was at work making small talk, she suspected, in order to give his brain time to get used to the overwhelming news she'd just dumped on him.

"I speak French, German and Italian fluently. And I can make my needs known in a few other languages, too." She smiled. "You never know where you'll be when you need to use the facilities."

His dark head bobbed, but she was uncertain just how much of this he was taking in.

"So, that's where you live? Lantanya?"

"No," she said, "actually my country is Lextanya. It's a smaller island across the strait from Lantanya. Though we're a protectorate of Lantanya. My father is Prince Wilhelm Adolf von Husden."

He nodded vaguely, prompting, "So that would make you…"

"Princess Catherine von Husden."

Riley looked as if the smallest touch of a feather just might knock him over.

"I know it's a lot to take in."

Again he nodded, and Catherine wanted to reach over to offer a comforting touch. But she didn't dare because she feared he might shake off her hand. He might come out of that stuporlike state and shout and rail at her. He had every right to be upset that she hadn't told him the full truth about who and what she was.

Riley seemed to be looking out the window, but Catherine suspected he wasn't actually seeing anything. His thoughts were most probably in utter chaos at the moment. His forehead would crease, then smooth, then crease again, as he evidently worked everything out in his head.

"And you say you're to be married?" he asked.

"Étienne is in Lextanya now awaiting my return. Father tracked me down here. He called my hotel and said he plans to announce my engagement at the weekend."

Some pieces snapped into place. "You said last night that you're leaving. You're going home today. And this is why."

It wasn't a question. Discomfort skulked around her shoulders. "Yes." She sighed. Softly, she said, "My flight leaves at midnight."

His features drew tight. "Didn't you say that you and your father don't have the greatest of relationships?"

Uncertain of where he was going, Catherine just looked at him.

"You led me to believe," he continued, "that your relationship was strained. In fact, you said you felt he didn't like you."

Anxiety started her foot swaying to and fro.

"You trust him to choose a husband for you?" Before she could respond, he twisted in the chair, swinging his gaze on to her. "And is that really done these days? Parents arranging marriages for their grown children?"

True bewilderment sharpened the angles of his face.

"It's a pretty common practice in my world."

He leaned against the chair back, clearly amazed. "So you're really a princess? Like real royalty?"

Reality was slowly sinking in.

"Yes."

"And being a princess is the reason you said you couldn't work? That you couldn't have a career?"

"That's right." He was thinking back over their time together, fitting together the puzzle. "I can volunteer all I want. But my taking a real job would be seen in my country as displacing someone who truly needs that job."

His head tilted. "Do you live in a castle?"

She grinned. "A massive one, made of stone and complete with turrets. Although much of it now has been converted into a museum where our people can come and see the accomplishments we've made throughout history. Still, though, our living quarters are quite spacious. I have a nice suite of rooms all to myself. You'd probably call it more of an apartment, I guess."

"Do you actually wear a crown?"

"No crown." One corner of her mouth quirked. "But I do have a diamond tiara that I wear to public functions. It was my great-grandmother's. Yvonne, my sister, talked Father into having a new one made for her, and it's a pretty elaborate headpiece. But I'm happy with great-grandma's tiara. However, I don't wear it often."

"A princess," he murmured under his breath.

Yes, the idea really was sinking in.

"But you didn't call your father a king. You called him Prince something or other."

Prince something or other? Wouldn't that just infuriate her father? Catherine stifled the bubble of laughter gathering at the back of her throat.

"Prince Wilhelm," she provided. "Lextanya has a conglomeration of complicated and ancient laws that connect us to Lantanya. The King of Lantanya—that would be my cousin Max—is the actual sovereign head of state of both islands. But my father is acting chief of state whenever Max isn't actually in Lextanya."

"Ah, so your father is like Prince John in *Robin Hood?*" She laughed. "The evil Prince John—"

"I meant no disrespect," he rushed to say.

"I know you didn't." Catherine thought a moment, then she said, "I think Father would rather be compared to Prince Rainier the Third of Monaco. Both men are monarchs. They make the laws along with their counsels, they rule the land and the people, but they'll never hold the title of king."

Riley sat quietly, taking it all in. When he tipped up his chin, she could tell his mind was in utter turmoil once again.

"Well, how does it work?" he asked. "The marriage arranging, I mean. It seems strange to me. How do royals go about finding husbands for their daughters? Come to think of it, is the arranging done only for daughters, or for sons, too? Are the arrangements made with the, um, prospective groom's parents or with the man, himself? Do you get to have any say in who is chosen? And why now? I mean, is there some kind of law that says you have to be married by a certain age? And if you don't do as you're told, is there some terrible consequence you must face? And—"

"Wait, wait." The query avalanche made her chuckle. She'd have to take this one question at a time. "First off, the idea isn't all that odd. All royals have arranged marriages for themselves and for their children at one time or another throughout history. It was—and continues to be— a means of elevating not just your family, but your entire country. After all, a marriage can make or break an entire nation. But the custom *is* changing, albeit slowly. Some royals have stopped the practice altogether. It depends a great deal, I think, on the open-mindedness of past and present generations. And their willingness to, um, keep up with the times." Her mouth twisted as she added, "Obviously the von Husden family—at least, my branch of it—has remained all too provincial. It doesn't help a bit that my father is a complete control freak. You wouldn't believe the pressure he's been putting on me lately. And we can't forget the Caslow diamond. Étienne's family owns it, and they've offered it to my father in exchange for my hand in marriage."

Realizing she was getting off on a tangent, she reeled herself in. "Anyway, the custom of choosing a mate is based on many unwritten rules, and those rules can vary for each kingdom. My father can't really force me to marry anyone—" she winced "—I think. You have to understand that this is a way of life for me. Marrying a man, giving birth to 'an heir and a spare' is simply my fate."

She lifted one shoulder. "My father has been orchestrating a match with one man or another ever since I turned twenty-one. I've come up with one excuse after the other to refuse the arrangements. But time is running out. And if he were to actually announce my official engagement—which he is threatening to do come Sunday—I don't see a way to get out of the commitment without causing my father, my whole family, a huge amount of embarrassment."

"Why now, though?" he repeated. "If he's been pressing you for years, and you've been avoiding it for years, why is there such urgency now?"

"It's Yvonne, my sister. She's agreed to a match." Catherine tucked her bottom lip between her teeth for a moment. "But she's younger than I. Being the oldest, I have

to marry first. It's protocol. One of those unwritten rules.
But this one is strict. There's no getting around it. Yvonne
has been waiting for nearly a year. She's pressuring Father,
and Father is pressuring me. He expects me to be on that
plane tonight. There's a party planned for Saturday night,
and an engagement luncheon set for Sunday."

"You're really going to go through with this?"

Catherine thought about her phone conversation with
her father, recalled the sound of his voice. "I think I've
pushed my father as far as he can be pushed."

"And this man you're to marry...this Étienne. Have you
even met him?"

She nodded. "The world I live in might be opulent by
your standards, but it's fairly small, and the people are few
who travel in the same circles as..."

"As royalty?" he provided.

Her head dipped. "It sounds so arrogant and pretentious." She didn't like thinking she was either of those
things.

"I've met him," she forced herself to continue. "But I
don't know him well."

"How is he going to feel when he discovers that you're
no longer—" He cut off the remainder of his sentence. He
tried again. "That you and I—"

Again, he was unable to put his thought into words, but
that was all right. Catherine knew well enough what he
meant.

She shrugged. She didn't know the answer to Riley's
question. And she didn't care, really.

"If he expected to marry a virtuous woman," she commented dryly, "then I think he should have been a little
more discreet in his own behavior, if you know what I
mean."

Riley shot her a knowing look. "He's got a reputation? He's a womanizer?"

Her brows arched. "He's known far and wide."

The idea seemed to trouble him, but he didn't say more. Finally, he said, "My God, Catherine. You're a von Husden. With an honest-to-goodness royal title."

Ah, she thought. The idea wasn't only sinking in, he was actually getting used to it.

His dark eyes leveled on her. "You don't want to marry this man."

He wasn't really asking. He knew her well for having known her such a short time.

She quietly told him, "I can't see any way out of it. It's what's expected of me."

Riley heaved a sigh as he scrubbed his fingers over his jaw. "The only good solution I can see to your problem happens to be the simplest one."

Solution? To suggest this was a problem with a *good* solution inferred that she had a choice in the matter. She'd lived her whole life with the idea that the very nature of who and what she was left her with no options whatsoever.

"I thought avoiding the whole sordid mess for as long as possible was the best solution I could hope for," she muttered. "The problem can't be avoided any longer."

"Sure it can."

Catherine stared at him.

"Just don't marry him."

Eleven

The look on Catherine's face convinced Riley that she thought he'd just made the most outlandish and rebellious suggestion in history. The idea wasn't in the least bizarre from where he was sitting. But he guessed it would be pretty hard for someone in her position to contemplate becoming a rebel.

A princess! He could hardly wrap his mind around the thought. The woman he'd been seeing, the woman he'd slept with was a royal.

In a flash, his thoughts turned inward, to last night.

Having her naked body curled up next to him had been one hell of a way to wake up. The warm, womanly scent of her had filled his nostrils, and her hair had draped across his chest. The soft rhythm of her breathing had been calming. Like gentle music soothing his soul.

And then the wonder filling him had escalated when he

remembered the awesome moments they'd spent making love. Catherine had rocked him to the core. She'd responded to him as if his touch contained a potent magic that carried her off to euphoria. The melodious moans that had issued from her luscious lips had driven him mad with need.

His mouth had gone dry just lying there thinking about it. It went dry again right now.

But then he recalled the instant he'd entered her. Pain had seemed to spear through her, and she'd gasped. He'd gone still, recognizing instantly what had been happening. The hazy passion had cleared in that instant, and he'd been prepared to stop right there and then. But she'd urged him onward. She'd crooned to him, stroked him with velvety fingers, kissed him with that searing mouth. And he'd surrendered to the desire surging through him, through them both.

Realizing what he'd done, what he'd taken from Catherine, had turned that wonderful, sleepy moment into a horrific recollection. Who the hell was he to take what she'd been keeping safe from all others for so long?

Yes, she'd coaxed him along, urged him on. But that didn't matter. She was an innocent. Her virginity was proof of that. She was inexperienced in such matters. He should have had the strength to stop. He should have crawled out of her bed, gotten himself dressed and left her hotel room.

But he hadn't.

Anger directed nowhere but at himself had begun to roil and seethe. Finally, he'd slid from beneath the sheets and had searched around for the clothes they had tossed hither and yon.

Catherine had awakened, seemingly unaware of his anguish. He'd gotten out of there as quickly as possible.

Then he'd arrived at the clinic, and his anger had been further whipped up by David Graham. The man's discriminatory management style was going to get him into big trouble one day. And Riley hadn't minced words when he'd told Dr. Graham just that.

Riley felt doubly guilty for leveling all that fury on Catherine when she'd shown up. He'd had no right to do it, and it wasn't as if he were really angry with her. He'd been the one in the wrong.

However, like a pin pricking a balloon, she'd taken all the wind—and anger—out of him when she'd disclosed her mind-boggling revelation.

A princess!

The idea continued to astound him.

Her blue eyes had clouded with such vulnerability when she had related her predicament that Riley had wanted desperately—once he'd finally wrapped his brain around the whole concept—to help her find a way out of her terrible fate.

What exactly had he meant when he'd blurted out the suggestion that she defy her father by not marrying the man who'd been chosen for her?

Come on, Riley, a voice in the back of his brain jeered, why don't you just fess up? You'd love to become Catherine's soldier of fortune, her shining knight. You'd love to rush in and rescue her from this awful dilemma.

How? By carrying her off to some fantasyland where she would be free of worry and strife forevermore?

What whimsical malarkey!

Whimsical or not, he could easily see them together. Hell, he'd love to wake up every morning next to Catherine! What man wouldn't?

But if he contemplated being with her, seriously, then

that meant he must also contemplate telling her the full truth about himself and the things he'd done.

That would be impossible.

He wasn't a soldier of anything. And he sure as hell was no shining knight. He was simply an ex-offender who was striving to rise above his tainted past.

How would Catherine—or worse yet, her family—react to *that* bit of news?

Well, they wouldn't get the chance to react. Not if he had any say in the matter. And he had all the say, he suddenly realized. Because he intended to see to it that Catherine would never find out.

Evidently, the lovely Catherine was unable to come up with a response to his suggestion. She sat on the couch looking as tense as a canary in a room full of tomcats.

Riley suddenly felt as if he'd overstepped his bounds. In fact, the advice he'd offered now seemed too simplistic, made it seem as if he thought her situation was easily avoided. And he didn't think that at all. He couldn't imagine the anguish she must be experiencing.

Little by little, the very air seemed to congeal with awkwardness.

The phone rang, and simultaneously there was a knock on Riley's door. An orderly poked his head into the office.

"Sorry to interrupt, but Dr. Lassen told me you're taking over for her today," the elderly gentleman said to Riley.

Rising to his feet, Riley said, "Yes, I am."

"I've got several requisition forms that need signing. I can't order supplies until I get a signature."

"I'll be right there." Riley glanced at Catherine once they were alone. Over the ringing of the phone, he said, "I'm sorry, but I promised Faye I'd—"

"I understand." She stood.

Riley couldn't let things end like this. "I'd like to see you this evening before you go. Would you have dinner with me tonight?"

She flinched as the phone rang a third time. She nodded. "I'd like that," she said, backing toward the door.

The fourth ring of the phone had Riley jerking the receiver to his ear and barking a none-too-pleasant greeting. He was barely aware of what the caller was saying as he watched Catherine disappear from his office.

"Well, don't think just because you're a princess," Faye said dryly, "that I intend to treat you any differently."

Catherine laughed. "That's exactly what I was hoping for."

She was amazed by how well Faye took the news. Why, the woman barely batted an eye.

"You've told Riley?"

Catherine nodded. "This morning."

The two women were enjoying a quick cup of tea late Friday afternoon in their favorite café around the corner from the clinic. Because Faye had been busy in the lab with Dr. Richie all day, she hadn't been able to make the lunch date with Catherine, so the women had arranged to meet as soon as Faye had finished at the lab for the day.

"Ah, so that was the problem," Faye said. "The chill radiating off Riley was so bad when we met in the hall that he could have been crowned the ice king."

Pursing her lips self-consciously, Catherine decided not to correct Faye regarding why Riley was upset when they met in the hallway earlier today.

"So he didn't take the news well?"

The porcelain handle of her teacup was cool against

Catherine's fingers. She didn't want to go into why Riley had been so curt when they'd all met up that morning. "Well, he didn't take it as well as you, I must say. He was overwhelmed. He had tons of questions."

Faye swirled sugar into her tea with a spoon. "Oh, there's plenty I'm dying to know. But I don't want to look like a commoner."

The snort Faye purposely emitted was most unlady-like, and it made Catherine laugh.

"Besides," Faye continued, "the way I figure it, we're going to be little ol' blue-haired ladies together, so I have the rest of my life to ask questions."

Catherine felt a rush of relief, and she reached over to slide her fingertips over her friend's forearm.

"I can't tell you how happy it makes me to hear you say that," she murmured, suddenly serious.

Bewilderment knit Faye's delicate brow. "Would you stop that? What did you think? I would stop being your friend because…"

Evidently, Catherine's expression caused Faye to let the rest of her thought wither away.

"Catherine?"

Catherine sighed. "I know it's probably hard to imagine, but so many people have ulterior motives." She pressed her lips together. "Let's just say that it's hard to find friends. *True* friends."

Faye set down her cup and covered Catherine's hand with her own. "I'm a true friend, Catherine."

The women basked in the heartrending moment, and Catherine feared she was going to tear up.

Finally, Faye said, "Are you really going to marry this Étienne?"

"I don't know," Catherine groaned. She leaned back in

her chair, tucked her hands in her lap. "If it turns out that I have to, would you be my maid of honor?"

"No way."

Faye's flat refusal shocked Catherine. Faye just shrugged.

"Didn't we just establish that I'm your true friend? My conscience wouldn't allow me to stand in some church, wearing some god-awful bridesmaid gown, knowing you were doing something you don't want to do."

Catherine smiled warmly. Then she whispered, "I was saving the god-awful gown for my sister."

They shared a chuckle.

"I agree with Riley about this, Catherine," Faye told her. "Don't do it."

Catherine rested her elbow on the table, her chin on her fist, worry over what she should or shouldn't do crowding her thoughts. She wished she had the answer. Sure it was fun to dream up all sorts of fairy tales. But reality was reality. There was no getting around it. Étienne was in Lextanya waiting for her return. And her father expected her to announce her engagement this very weekend.

"Did Riley have any other wisdom to offer?" Faye asked.

She shook her head. "We ran out of time. The phone started ringing, and someone came knocking on his door."

"Poor man." One corner of Faye's mouth quirked wickedly. "He had no idea what he was getting himself into when he offered to cover my schedule today. I saw him just before I left the clinic, and he was exhausted."

"I hope he's not too tired." Catherine absently smoothed the linen napkin that was spread across her lap. "He promised to have dinner with me this evening. Our last hurrah before I have to leave."

Anguish shadowed Faye's gaze. "Don't go, Catherine." Her voice packed a concentrated punch when she quietly added, "I imagine being married to a man you don't love has got to be just as bad as loving a man you can't be with."

Empathy wrenched Catherine's insides when she thought of the pain Faye lived with every day because of her broken relationship with her husband, Mark. The urge to say something comforting welled up in Catherine, but it was quickly swamped by the need to pass on some earnest advice.

"Faye," she began, but then, uncertain as to how her opinion would be met, she clamped her lips shut.

"True friends can say what they want, Catherine, because it comes from the heart."

Catherine offered her a small smile. "What I was going to say was maybe you just think you can't be with Mark. Maybe there is a way for you to be with the man you love."

Faye looked at her. She picked up the dainty cup sitting on the table and took a sip of her tea. As she set the cup back on its saucer, Faye leveled a serious gaze on to Catherine.

"Could be," Faye said gently, "that advice is something you need to pay close attention to, as well. You think?"

Riley was unlocking his car when Richard Strong hailed him from several yards away.

"Dr. Richie," Riley greeted, shaking the man's hand when he reached him, "how did it go in the lab today?"

"Great! Just great! Listen, I'd like for you to call me Richard, if you would."

"Sure. No problem. Call me Riley."

"I happened to see you out here and I wanted to catch you before you left. To thank you."

Riley couldn't think of what he might have done to warrant this.

"For treating me so well. Accepting me back into the fold, I guess you could say. A lesser man might have used the fact that he'd taken over my job to—" he lifted a shoulder "—well, to play lord of the manor. But you didn't. You've treated me respectfully and I appreciate that."

"It's clear you put a lot of hard work into NoWait," Riley said. "I felt all along that if the oil was going to be tested, you should be in on it."

Richard's gaze darted, and he shifted his weight from one foot to the other. He looked at Riley. "I'd like to know if you'd help me out with something."

"I'll do what I can."

"I suggested to Dr. Graham today that I give a seminar."

"I remember." Riley hadn't thought it was a good idea then, and he still didn't. The people who visited the clinic no longer trusted Dr. Richie.

"Well," Richard continued, "I had a chance to walk around a bit today and I talked to some of the clients." His tone lowered as he admitted, "Those who didn't avoid me, anyway."

Absently, Riley shifted his briefcase over to his left hand, his attention focused on Richard.

"I'm not sure my seminar would be very well received at the moment."

Riley could tell this was a difficult admission for the man.

"The people around here have really lost faith in me."

Although it would be hard to voice the truth, Riley felt that if the situation were reversed and he were the one in Richard's shoes, the truth was exactly what he would want.

In as kind a voice as possible he said, "Richard, leaving the clinic the way you did is bound to come with a few consequences. But you'll get back on your feet. Give it time."

Riley wasn't lying. He'd met many a Richard Strong in his life, charismatic people who took a misstep into a huge pile of manure, but still managed to come out of it smelling like a rose.

"I was hoping you might talk to Dr. Graham," Richard said. "Convince him that I ought to lay low for a while. Persuade him to let me stay in the lab for now. I'd suggest it myself, but then I'd have to go into reasons and motivations and whatnot. And to tell you the truth, I'd rather not have to admit to him what I just admitted to you. About the clients having lost faith, I mean. I already look bad enough in his eyes, you know?"

Riley just nodded. "I'll talk to Dr. Graham. I'll make him understand about the seminar."

"Thanks. And one more thing," he said. "About my stepping back into my original position here at the clinic…"

Oh, Lord. Riley hoped Richard didn't expect him to go to bat for him, because he had no intention of doing that.

"I'm, uh, not sure I'm the right man for the job."

Riley was unable to quell his surprise.

"Don't get me wrong," Richard rushed to explain. "It's not that I'm not grateful. The clinic has been great to me. But I've been thinking about something all day…something amazing."

The man's eyes took on a strange quality.

"If the testing goes well," Richard said, "if NoWait proves to be a true all-natural homeopathic aphrodisiac, the oil just might launch me into the big time. I could be the male Dr. Ruth of the new millennium. I could be famous."

Riley finally figured out the look in Richard's eyes. Visions of grandeur were sparkling so brightly. He sure had lofty ideas. But then again, Riley figured, no famous person became famous without them.

"I heard from Faye today that you don't intend to stay on as director at the clinic," Richard said.

"That's right. I'm only here temporarily."

"That's too bad," he murmured. "Maybe you could break it to Dr. Graham that I'm not the best person for the job."

"I can do that." Riley hoped he hadn't responded too quickly. He held no animosity toward Richard. He simply felt that Faye was a better candidate. She'd been running the clinic right from the start and she deserved to become director. Hell, she deserved to become the clinic's new chief.

"Well, that's great," Richard said, clearly feeling pleased with the way the conversation had gone. "I'd better get going. My son's flying into town later tonight. He's nineteen. A student at UCLA." A huge smile took over his face. "Jason and I have never met, so tonight is going to be pretty exciting for me."

He reached out his hand, and Riley took it.

"Good luck," Riley said.

"Thanks. For everything." Richard inhaled deeply, his chest puffing. He looked around him and announced, "Yes, things are really looking up."

Catherine packed her suitcase with a heavy heart. She didn't want to go home. She truly didn't.

She'd have loved nothing more than to follow Riley's advice. Advice that Faye agreed with. However, neither of them understood the magnitude of the problem.

The von Husden sovereigns had been choosing spouses for their progeny for hundreds of years. It was tradition. Tight and binding custom. This wasn't something she could just shirk off.

Well, she might be able to get away with not marrying Étienne. If she went on a hunger strike and closed herself off in her rooms, her father might relent. But Prince Wilhelm would not be put off forever. He'd find another suitor. And with Yvonne champing at the bit to marry Hampstead, their father would come up with another available man for his Fat Cat posthaste—and that one might be a real slime-bucket.

But whether she decided to marry Étienne or not, she *had* to be on the plane when it left at midnight or her father really would announce her engagement on Sunday. And then the whole deal would pretty much be signed, sealed and delivered. A pronouncement made by the prince himself was almost as binding as law.

Catherine sat on the side of the bed and scrubbed her fingers over her cheeks.

You've ached for Father's love and approval all your life, a tiny voice in her head whispered. If you go home, as he's asked…if you marry Étienne, as he's asked, then you'll have the very thing you've been seeking for so long.

Her hands sank to the mattress and she sighed. Unwittingly, she smoothed her palms over the soft bedspread. In an instant, images, raw and reckless, blazed though her mind.

She and Riley naked and writhing on this very bed.

She and Riley caressing and kissing.

She and Riley seemingly unable to get enough of each other, but bound and determined to try.

When Catherine lifted her hand she saw that her fingers

were trembling. Heat sprouted to life deep inside her, and the memory of Riley's touch, of his fiery kisses, made her grow moist and needy in the most womanly and wanton part of her.

That was the kind of irresistible passion she longed to share with the man with whom she took eternal vows. That was the kind of hungry fervor she wanted to experience with her husband.

Not for one night. But for the rest of her life.

Was that too much to ask?

Her grandmother, her mother, even her sister might be willing to settle for a lifetime stuck in a cold and unfeeling union with men they had neither chosen nor loved. But Catherine had been fighting against the notion for years.

Sure, the older women in her family had tried to argue that arranged marriages made for a more settled life, a more secure existence, because you knew what you were getting into—what was expected of you—from the very beginning. Catherine's grandmother had even contended that she and her husband, Catherine's beloved grandfather, had grown to be very fond of each other. And Catherine's mother had challenged Catherine to name a single time she'd ever seen her parents fussing or fighting.

Catherine couldn't. Because they didn't fight. There was no animosity between them. But neither, Catherine suspected, was there any passion.

Her parents were simply two people who happened to cohabitate.

Catherine shivered, the mere idea filling her with a vast emptiness.

Absently, she picked up one of the silky blouses lying beside her leather suitcase. It felt as if it weighed ten pounds. She stuffed it in haphazardly with the other clothes she'd already packed.

Riley's suggestion entered her mind, unbidden.

Just don't marry him, he'd told her.

Catherine chuckled despite the heaviness of her heart. Riley was an intelligent man. Hadn't that been one of the reasons she'd been attracted to him when they'd first met? That, and his grumpiness. Yes, the fact that he'd been short with her had actually stirred her interest. It had made her wonder what was going on in that mind of his. It had made her want to find out why he was so hesitant to smile.

But what she'd found out was that he wasn't as gruff as he led those around him to believe. Before long she'd had him grinning and teasing and, yes, even flirting with her.

What is it you're looking for? he'd asked her.

She'd wanted him to want her. And if she'd had more time to spend in Portland with Riley, she was nearly certain that they would have ended up just where they'd ended up last night. In her bed. In each other's arms. In sheer and utter ecstasy. Without the help of NoWait.

Nearly certain.

Nearly.

Her hand stilled on the handle of the suitcase. Had the NoWait really helped her get what she wanted? It had caused her to accomplish what she'd gone after—Riley's uncontrollable passion for her. But...

The thoughts came slowly as she tried to work them out in her head.

But what she'd wanted was for him to want her, for him to make the first move. Instead, the oil she'd smoothed onto her skin had taken the choice out of his hands by inducing him, drugging him.

What had she done? She hadn't gotten what she wanted

from Riley. Not at all. Why hadn't she realized how using that oil would ruin everything?

Because you didn't take the time to think, the voice in her head accused. You only acted on your own selfish wishes.

Catherine flung herself back on the mattress, steeped in misery. She'd manipulated Riley. The man she loved.

Her eyes went wide and she stared at the stark white ceiling.

She pressed her hands flat against her solar plexus.

She loved Riley?

Yes, she loved him!

Such a revelation would usually make a woman elated. But she groaned like a wounded animal, turned onto her side and curled into a fetal position. She'd tricked the man she loved into making love with her.

How had she made such a terrible mess of things? She hadn't meant to. All the saints in heaven knew that.

Well, there was no getting around it. She had to try to straighten this out. She had to try to correct her wrongs. If she didn't, she wouldn't be able to live with herself.

The first course of action in making things right was telling Riley about the NoWait.

Twelve

Carrie Martin's heart pinched with poignant emotion as she watched Richard prowl from one end of her small living room to the other. Every time he reached the picture window, he peeked out into the night.

"We should have gone to the airport to pick him up." Richard turned to face Carrie and the window sheer settled back into place.

"Jason's very independent. He always has been." The pent-up energy was more than she could stand. "Would you relax? You're making me nervous."

"Sorry," he muttered. "But I can't help it. I don't think I've ever been this edgy." He tossed her a lopsided grin. "But it's a good kind of edgy, you know?"

Carrie nodded. "Come sit down."

"What kind of kid was he?" Richard eased down onto the sofa next to her. "What did he like to do?"

"It would be easier to tell you what he didn't like to do," she said. "He was into everything. From the time he was a toddler, he was curious and energetic."

Richard reclined against the sofa's back and hooked one ankle over his knee.

"He walked and talked early," Carrie continued. "I never had trouble finding sitters. Everyone just loved him. He was the life of the party wherever he went." She grinned. "And if there wasn't an actual party, he made one, on the spot."

"That's my boy."

She couldn't help but chuckle at the pride in Richard's voice. Softly she commented, "From the day he was born, he was the image of you, Richard. He still is."

A memory from the past made her grin. "Once I came strolling through the living room and saw him with all these nuts and screws and metal pieces laid out in front of him. He was studying them with a fierce concentration. I was about to ask him what he was doing, when I realized he'd taken apart the doorbell.

"I started to scold him." Her tone lowered. "'I wanted to know how it worked, Mommy,' he said." The touching recollection made her smile. "I waggled my finger right in front of his little nose and told him he'd better put it back just the way he found it."

"And did he?"

Carrie shrugged. "Not quite. One of the chimes clunked a little after that, but I didn't mind."

"Oh, my," Richard said on a sigh. "Sounds like he was an awesome kid."

"He was. He listened to me, never talked back. He didn't keep his room the cleanest, but he did okay. He liked grade school. Did really well, too. And he played sports—baseball, football, soccer. You name it, Jason gave it a go. And so many parents complain about their boys when they get to be teens. But he hasn't given me a single minute of trouble. Not one, Richard. I'm so lucky."

Carrie realized that her ex had grown very quiet. Her gaze lifted to his, and the regret she saw clouding his dark eyes made her feel terribly guilty.

"Oh, Richard," she said, "I'm sorry. You've missed so much. So very much. I shouldn't have gone on and on like that."

He sat up, reached out and touched her shoulder. "Don't be silly. I want to know. I want to know everything."

The heat of him penetrated the fabric of her blouse. Their eyes met, and held. The intensity between them seemed too much, too fast. Feeling suddenly perplexed, Carrie turned away.

Richard let his hand slide from her shoulder, and he placed it in his lap.

Awkwardness laced the edges of the room.

"Tell me something."

There was a forced boisterousness in his words, but Carrie didn't mind because she knew he was attempting to get past the unexpected discomfort they'd gotten tangled up in.

"Was your second husband good to Jason?"

Immediately, Carrie relaxed. "Ralph was a good father, Richard. He was patient and kind. Never raised his voice. Never had to. Oh, he made Jason toe the line. He was a disciplinarian. Parents have to be, or children would just go wild. But Ralph wasn't overly strict."

Getting caught up in memories of what felt like a whole different lifetime, she absently smoothed her hand across the worn chenille throw that was draped across the arm of the couch.

"Before we married," she continued, "he sat me down and asked me just how involved I wanted him to be in my son's life. I told him I felt that Jason needed a father, in every sense of the word, and if he were so inclined to be that kind of father, then I was all for it." She pictured her deceased husband's face, grief tweaking at her insides. "And he became Jason's father. In every sense of the word.

"Ralph couldn't do a thing without Jason tagging along after him. They camped and fished. Ralph took him to his baseball games. Even if Ralph was just tinkering out in the garage, Jason would be out there, too."

She went quiet. Finally, she tipped up her chin, realizing that she'd gotten lost in all that wonderful, wholesome pleasantness.

"He was a good man," she assured Richard. "I know that your raising Jason would probably have been the best-case scenario. But since that wasn't possible, Ralph did a darned good job of loving our son and bringing him up to be a fine young man."

Richard looked pensive. "I'll always be grateful to Ralph Martin for being there for Jason when I wasn't, Carrie. Because I don't know what kind of a father I'd have been to the boy."

"Oh, now—"

Richard cut her off with a lift of his hand. "No, now's not the time for lies. I've been trying lately to face the cold hard facts about who and what I was…who and what I am." He paused, then added, "Who and what I want to be."

Carrie wasn't sure what to say, so she didn't say anything.

"We both know I was pretty self-centered." He barked out a single, humorless laugh. "I was headstrong, too. I didn't want to settle down. I wanted one thing: to make a name for myself. I didn't care about anything else. I didn't care about you. I didn't care about our marriage. At least, not enough. And because of that—"

His dark eyes latched on to hers and Carrie felt something akin to electric current thrum in the air.

"—I lost the best thing I ever had." He moistened his lips. "You."

Some kind of magnetic energy held her spellbound. She hadn't felt this kind of awareness in many, many years.

Oh, she'd loved Ralph. They'd had a wonderful marriage filled with many happy and fulfilling years. But there had always been a part of her that had missed Richard. He had a charismatic way about him, a compelling charm that was captivating. He made her tingle from the top of her head to the tips of her toes.

"I wouldn't have been good for Jason," Richard said. "If you think about it, if you let yourself honestly remember the kind of person I was back then, you'll have to agree."

He shook his head in derision. "Back then, nothing! I'm still a no-good son of a bitch. Just today at the clinic I was suggesting to Dr. Jacobs that if NoWait turns out to be a true aphrodisiac, it could very well make me a famous man." Anguish bit into his brow. "What is *wrong* with me, Carrie?"

"There is nothing wrong with being ambitious." Without thinking about it, she reached out and took his hand in hers. "You happen to be very motivated, determined to make something of yourself. I think that's…admirable."

She'd been about to use a more intimate word, but caught herself. Feeling drawn by Richard's charisma might be beyond her control, but she didn't have to act on it. He'd given her several looks that had seemed to communicate some warm and luscious messages. But this man had hurt her. No, he'd crushed her. She had to remember that and keep her heart as safe as possible.

Of course, she realized that she'd had a hand in the failure of their marriage all those years ago, but still, there was no need to reveal the attraction buzzing inside her—bare her soul, so to speak—until he made plain his intentions.

The silent vibrations seemed to whir at a higher resonance, and there was no mistaking the fact that Richard noticed it, too.

He gently tightened his hold on her hand, his palm secure against hers. "Carrie, we were so young back then. I messed things up royally—"

"*We* messed things up," she corrected. Immediately, she regretted her rashness and wondered if she'd revealed too much. No, she quickly decided, she was only telling him the truth.

The weighty pause that followed seemed crucial and gave them both some needed time to reflect.

"So much time has passed." Richard's voice sounded rusty and grating. "And I know it probably isn't fair of me to bring this up. But I can't help it. All the time that I was away from the clinic, I was going over and over things. My whole life has been filled with a constant stream of empty relationships. I kept remembering when we were together. How dedicated you were, how devoted, how committed—"

"Stop, Richard. You're making me sound like a saint." She tried to laugh, but couldn't. "And I was no saint. Believe me."

He was clearly bewildered.

"I got pregnant on purpose," she blurted. "I intentionally stopped taking my birth control pills. I was trying to force your hand. I thought a baby would make you settle down." Guilt and anguish tightened her throat until she thought she'd suffocate. "I knew I was pregnant the night I gave you that ultimatum. And I almost told you." The magnitude of her angst had her repeating, "I almost told you. But you were so angry, and I couldn't believe how everything was falling apart."

He slid closer and took her in his arms. There was nothing sexual in his caress, and she gratefully rested her head against his shoulder.

"Oh, Carrie," he crooned. "We are a pair, aren't we?"

She didn't bother answering what she knew was a rhetorical question.

Her voice was small as she said, "We need to start out slowly. Very slowly."

He smiled. She didn't have to see his face to know it; she felt it.

"As you said, so much time has passed," she told him. "We need to get to know each other. We need to become friends...first."

She'd wanted to say they needed to become friends before they could become lovers, but she couldn't get those words out.

"There are so many problems." She flattened her palm against his chest and lifted her head to look up into his handsome face. "There are six hundred miles between San Francisco and Portland. I have a teaching job I have to return to, Richard. And then there's—"

"Shhh." The touch of his index finger was tender against her mouth. "We'll work all that out, Carrie. As you said, we'll take it slow."

The phone jangled and made her jump. She got up to answer it.

Carrie listened to the voice on the line, horror pervading her as her whole world rolled off-kilter.

Realizing something was very wrong, Richard went to her. "What is it, Carrie? What's the matter?"

"The taxi Jason hired was involved in an accident." She dropped the phone receiver into its cradle. "Our son's been taken to Portland General."

Riley shook his head. "I just don't get it."

Morgan's Pub was located in downtown Portland. Riley had brought Catherine here because this had been one of his favorite haunts for years. The food was tasty and the owners prided themselves on their draft beer, the variety of which was unequaled in the city.

The atmosphere was as comfortable as an old, worn shoe, but Riley was too preoccupied to enjoy it tonight. Catherine had spent the past thirty minutes trying to make him understand her life as a royal. But he was quickly coming to the conclusion that he'd never appreciate what she was trying to explain.

Her title of princess offered her a world that was privileged, yes. But it also seemed restrictive. Sectarian. And terribly exclusionary.

No wonder Catherine had felt the need to flee Lextanya. If he'd been the one carrying the scepter, he'd have run away long ago. He was just surprised she'd held out so long.

Despondence weighed down the sigh Catherine exhaled. "Sitting here telling you this, even I think it sounds crazy. But it all seems so normal when you're living it. I was born into this, Riley. I've heard my mother refer to my father as 'The Prince' for as long as I can remember. If I wanted to visit my grandmother, I've always had to call her secretary and schedule an appointment."

"That sounds so cold." His comment sounded overly critical, but the thought had been voiced before he could stop it.

"But it's not," she insisted. "My grandmother loves me very much. It's just that she's got duties and responsibilities." Again, Catherine sighed.

The call of nature had Riley excusing himself. That and the fact that he could also use a moment to think. He got up from the table and weaved through the crowd toward the rear of the establishment.

He'd been surprised to hear Catherine tell him she'd packed and was ready for that midnight flight out of Portland. It's not that he expected her never to return home, but he didn't like the idea that she was pretty much being dictated to by her father.

Catherine had said she didn't intend to marry the man her father had waiting. But she'd also said that her father would only find someone else. Eventually, she'd have to marry one of the aristocratic Lotharios her father selected for her.

The rest-room door issued a loud squeak when he pushed it open.

She was going to shackle herself to a loveless marriage. For what?

He nodded absently at the heavyset man who was washing his hands at the sink. The guy swayed on his feet when he tipped his chin in greeting. Evidently the small movement threw off his balance and he lurched backward violently.

"Whoa, there!" Riley reached out to steady him. But rather than being appreciative of the help, the drunk swung out his arm.

"Get off, man."

The words were spoken slow and thick, and the stench of beer was so dense, Riley couldn't help but grimace.

"Whatever you say." Riley turned away, only to hear a scuffle. He twisted back around just in time to hear an "oof," the impact with the sink knocking the breath out of the guy. In an instant, Riley knelt at his side where the man had landed in a heap on the floor.

Before Riley could ask any questions, the drunk pushed himself onto his hands and knees. Riley helped him to stand.

"I tol' you to mine yer own biz wax, buddy."

"Seems like you've had more than your share tonight. Maybe you should go home and sleep it off."

That bit of advice elicited a vulgar response, and then the drunk pulled open the door and was gone. Riley just shook his head.

Back at the table, he slid onto the wooden bench across from Catherine. He'd only had about half of his beer, but his encounter in the rest room had spoiled his taste for the stuff and he slid it a few inches away.

"Now, where were we?" he asked. "Oh, yes. I was about to give you the lecture of a lifetime."

She grinned, sliding her fingers over the condensation on the outside of her glass. "I'm ready," she told him.

"You don't want to go home," he began with the flat-out fact of the matter. "I can see it in your eyes. So why go? You're a beautiful woman, Catherine. You're intelligent. You could marry any man you want." The feelings rushing through him were strange—dismay, sadness, distress, even anger. His gaze slid to the lit candle on the table, as he blurted out, "I don't understand why this is bugging me to this degree. You need to do what you feel is right for you. But if things were different—"

He nearly choked. What the hell was the matter with him? He'd reminded himself over and over again that Catherine wasn't the woman for him. Or rather, that he wasn't the man for her.

"Don't say anything more."

Her soft but urgent voice tugged at his attention and he lifted his eyes to hers. Oh, she needn't worry about that! He had no intention of saying more. No sir, he didn't.

"I have something to confess," she said. "Something about last night."

The abrupt about-face of the conversation took him aback. He was truly stumped as to what she might be going to say.

Catherine nibbled on her bottom lip, emotion clouding her features. "There's no easy way to say this, Riley. But my conscience is bothering me, so I just have to find a way. I have to be honest with you."

Her delicate shoulders rounded in what looked a lot like shame, and that only confused him more.

"As I told you, Riley, I've realized that I came to Portland looking for something. At first, I didn't even know what it was but now I know I wanted acceptance from someone who didn't know who I was."

"Acceptance?" Man, had she ever used the wrong word. His response was sharp as he continued, "This morning you were pretty clear that you wanted someone to want you, as in physical desire. Someone who was ignorant of your identity. Well, you succeeded on both counts, Catherine."

"But not without help."

Riley rested his forearms on the edge of the table and stared in silence. Not even the ruckus at a nearby table was enough to make him break eye contact with her.

Without another word, Catherine reached into her purse and pulled out a small blue vial and set it next to the salt and pepper shakers.

"What's that?"

"It's NoWait."

"No, it isn't. NoWait comes in two-ounce brown bottles and has a label that was designed by Dr. Strong. I've seen them."

Reluctantly, she declared, "This came from the lab. I went there and found trays of these. And black, leather-bound laboratory notebooks were sitting on the counter. NoWait was typed out on—"

"Catherine! What did you do?"

"I needed more time, Riley. I just needed more time. But I knew I had to leave—"

"What the hell have you done?"

Riley couldn't believe it. He hadn't been in the lab for days. He'd read the protocol, but he'd left most everything to Faye. He knew nothing about testing procedures. He knew the technicians were setting up the apparatus needed to begin the experiments, getting the oil ready to be tested. They must have measured out the NoWait into tiny blue vials like the one sitting on the table.

"You *used* that stuff? When I was at your hotel last night? Dammit, Catherine, you knew the oil was off-limits. I know for a fact that you knew it because I was the one who told you."

Her blue eyes glistened with tearful regret. She whispered, "I know you did."

Barraged with emotion, Riley sat there, stunned. Betrayed. Lied to. Misled. He felt all of those things. And anger. No, the heat rampaging through him wasn't mere anger, it was fury.

"You manipulated me, Catherine."

The sound of cutlery and dishes crashing to the wood floor drew all eyes toward a table on the far side of the pub. A woman let out a scream and a frightened waiter gaped toward the floor, shouting, "Sir? Sir?"

Riley sprang from his seat and hurried across the pub. He was vaguely aware that Catherine followed close on his heels.

Even before he reached the commotion, he began surveying the situation.

The man lying on the floor looked to be unconscious. Riley realized it was the heavyset drunk he'd met in the rest room just a few minutes before. The man didn't seem to be breathing.

The face of the young waiter was a ghostly white. He was obviously scared to death. When he caught sight of Riley, the kid seemed relieved that someone intended to offer help. A woman sat at the table, wailing and distraught.

"I'm a doctor," Riley announced.

"I thought he was choking," the waiter said. "I tried the Heimlich maneuver."

"He was conscious at the time?" Riley asked, getting down on his knees to get a closer look.

"Barely. But he was already turning blue."

"Was any food expelled?" Riley asked.

"No, sir. And he seemed to get worse. Quick." A tremor quivered his voice as he asked, "I didn't hurt him, did I?"

A man in a suit arrived. "I'm the manager. I've called nine-one-one."

"Good." Riley grasped the plackets of the man's shirt and gave a good yank. Buttons went flying.

Questions raced through Riley's head.

"Ma'am," he called out loudly over the woman's sobs, "does he have a heart condition?" When she didn't answer, he raised his voice louder. "Does he have other medical conditions that you know of? Is he currently taking medications?"

The woman was obviously too hysterical to help. The man's white T-shirt rolled up over his belly easily. Signs of an ugly bruise were clear high on the man's ribs where he'd hit the sink earlier.

Then Riley noticed something peculiar. Only one side of the man's chest showed signs of movement. He checked the man's pulse.

Rapid heartbeat. Bluish color. Distended neck veins.

"When I brought him that last double shot of bourbon a couple of minutes ago," the waiter offered, "I heard him complain that he had difficulty breathing. And then just a second ago when I was passing the table, he was turning blue."

Having seen the heavyset drunk fall in the rest room, Riley suspected he knew what the problem was, and he feared the kid's treatment for choking had only worsened the crisis. Palpation of the man's chest resulted in a spongy feeling beneath Riley's fingers. Respiratory emergencies called for immediate action.

"We've got to restore full oxygen flow to the heart and brain," Riley said, standing and scanning the tables around him, "or this guy's going to be in deep trouble."

He snatched up a clean steak knife and napkin from an unoccupied table. Then he picked up the cocktail glass from where his patient had been sitting. Riley glanced at the waiter. "Bourbon, you said?"

"That's right," the young man told him.

"You got a pen?"

The waiter plucked one from the pocket of his black apron.

The manager moved closer. "What are you going to do?"

"I'm going to help him breathe."

Working as swiftly as he could, Riley crouched and tucked one edge of the napkin under the man's side, arranging it to make himself a small work area. He placed the crude, makeshift scalpel on the white linen. He unscrewed the pen, setting the empty tube on the napkin and tossing aside the extraneous parts. He then poured about a half shot of the bourbon into his cupped palm and rubbed his hands together.

"Anything I can do?" the manager asked.

"Give me a sec. Then you can lend a hand." From the look on the manager's face, Riley suspected he was sorry he'd offered.

Riley splashed alcohol on the unconscious man's skin. Then he poured some bourbon on both the knife and the pen tube. "Here, take this." He handed the glass to the manager.

Carefully choosing a spot several inches below the man's armpit, Riley felt for the position of the ribs. With a confident and steady hand, he cut a small incision.

Blood welled, and the woman who'd been crying gasped and then went quiet. In fact, the whole dining room seemed to have grown eerily silent.

Riley focused. With firm pressure, he plunged the empty pen tube into the incision, sliding it between the ribs. Instantly, a whoosh of air whistled through the tube, confirming Riley's diagnosis.

"He was trying to breathe," he murmured, "but the air he inhaled was being trapped in the chest cavity. Had no way to expel itself."

Riley capped and uncapped the tube in synchrony with the man's breath. The blue tinge of the man's skin began to fade almost immediately.

After watching him for a few seconds, the restaurant manager's tone filled with astonishment as he softly asked, "You're actually exhaling for him?"

Riley nodded. "The EMTs will be able to do a better job of it once they arrive. They'll have the proper equipment."

As if on cue, the faint shrill of a siren approached from somewhere down the busy city block. Emergency lights flashed through the front windows of the pub as the ambulance pulled up at the front door.

"Everyone, back up," Riley called to the restaurant patrons. "Give the paramedics a little room to maneuver."

Suddenly, Riley remembered Catherine. He looked up and caught her gaze on his. Tension filled her beautiful face, and Riley had no idea if her stress was caused by the emergency situation or their very own personal calamity. He lost sight of her as the milling crowd cleared the area.

Dark emotions swam in his gut as he thought of her and what she'd done, but he thrust them out of his mind and looked down, concentrating on what he was doing.

Two EMTs shoved their way through the door. The manager stood and gave them a shout, and they zigzagged their way between the tables.

"What've we got?" The paramedic set down his trauma kit with a thump.

"Tension pneumothorax," Riley told him. "I witnessed the patient fall in the rest room earlier this evening. He struck his chest against the sink but he insisted he was all right. You should know he's pretty intoxicated. You have a chest tube?"

"Sure do."

It took several minutes for the paramedics to treat the patient. The manager brought Riley several hot, moist cloths so he could clean up some, and Riley thanked him.

The EMTs expertly inserted the chest tube and then they hooked it up to a portable, compact vacuum bottle. The vacuum made a low whir as it slowly and continuously removed the excess air from the man's pleural space. The paramedics prepared the unconscious man for transport, lifting him onto the stretcher and then securely fastening the straps.

"Thanks for your help," the paramedic finally said to Riley, sliding the trauma kit onto a metal platform beneath the stretcher.

"You're welcome. I'm just glad I was here." A split second later he added, "In fact, I think I'll follow you to the ER so I can talk to the doctor on duty."

The EMT just nodded and then wheeled the stretcher toward the front door of the pub where the ambulance waited.

A conscientious doctor, Riley wanted to make sure the man received good follow-up treatment. But as he made his way back to the table where Catherine sat waiting for him, he knew concern for the man he'd just treated wasn't the only reason he wanted to make a hasty exit. He wanted to avoid a confrontation with Catherine.

What she'd done was indefensible in his mind. Nothing she could say would cause him to excuse it. When he approached her, her features were drawn. She was pale, her eyes haunted.

"You were amazing, Riley," she said.

"Just doing what I was trained to do."

The NoWait still sat in the center of the table. His jaw was so tight it began to ache. "Listen, I'm going to go to

Portland General to make sure everything goes smoothly for that guy."

Catherine was almost too quick to nod.

"Want me to call you a taxi?"

"No," she said. "I'm close enough to my hotel to walk. It's a nice night. I'll be fine. You go ahead."

There would be no further discussion of the oil that sat there like an elephant in an OR being purposely unnoticed.

That was fine with him.

His gaze latched on to hers for several long seconds.

"Well, good luck, Catherine. With whatever you decide to do." He picked up his jacket from where it was draped over the back of the rustic bench. While he was still leaning toward the table, he reached out and swiped up the small blue vial of NoWait as inconspicuously as possible. Catherine didn't comment.

He told her, "I'll pay the tab on my way out."

There was panic in her expression. She wasn't happy with his goodbye. He could tell. However, he felt there simply wasn't anything else he could do except turn on his heel and walk away.

Thirteen

Catherine stood at the counter waiting for the hotel clerk to finalize her checkout bill. Her favorite bellman—an elderly black man named Andy whom she'd seen often over the course of her visit—hovered nearby with her two bags, ready to hail her a cab that would whisk her to the airport.

This holiday to Portland was supposed to have been filled with fun and adventure, yet she was leaving the city feeling more depressed and wretched than she had when she'd arrived. And she couldn't blame anyone but her own foolish self.

Oh, her stay hadn't been a total loss. She'd made a wonderful friend in Faye Lassen. She and Faye both had been close to tears when they'd said their goodbyes and parted company late this afternoon. But there was no doubt in Catherine's mind that she'd see Faye again, and that their friendship would continue.

And she'd learned a lot at the Healthy Living Clinic. The seminars she'd attended had offered her a slew of information about good nutrition, proper exercise and how to live a healthy life. Her time in the gym with the trainer had her feeling fit and firm. So the trip hadn't been a total bust.

But the gloom that swamped her returned full force when she thought of Riley and just how badly she'd mangled their relationship. She'd snuffed the very life out of it.

He'd been appalled by what she'd done. He'd felt betrayed. He couldn't have been blunter about that.

What she still couldn't figure out was why she'd acted so rashly. Sure, she'd felt the pressure of time. However, if that humiliating incident during her teen years had taught her anything, it was that she needed to think through all aspects and outcomes of her actions *before* she acted. That lesson had been worth its weight in gold throughout her life, and it had been worth all those forced hours of volunteerism her father—who had presided over the special judiciary council gathering—had sentenced her to back then.

The experience had engraved an indelible message on her brain. Yet, when it had come to Riley and the NoWait, she hadn't even allowed that hard-earned life lesson to enter her thoughts.

Why?

She accepted her receipt from the smiling receptionist and then turned to Andy.

"Guess I'm ready," she told him.

The man picked up her bags and started for the door. "Won't take a second to find you a cab." And just as he promised, Andy soon held open the rear passenger-side door of a taxi for her.

"I hope you enjoyed your stay, Miz Houston," Andy said.

She discreetly slipped him a generous tip. The sheer magnitude of her misery had her admitting, "I have to say I'd be feeling better about my visit if I hadn't treated a certain new friend so thoughtlessly. I was downright reckless."

The bellman's head tipped, and he grinned. "My mama always said that if a person has you acting crazy, you best take note. It means something."

Catherine smiled benignly and slid into the cab while Andy moved to the rear of the car to load her bags into the trunk.

Crazy was the perfect word to describe her behavior with Riley.

Wild. Idiotic. Senseless. And normally she was none of those things.

You best take note. Andy's mama's advice floated through Catherine's thoughts. *It means something.*

It means something.

He means something.

He means *everything.*

Catherine's spine went rod-straight.

Andy slammed shut the trunk and gave the top of it two sharp thumps with the palm of his hand as a signal to the cabbie that he could drive on.

In a flash, Catherine remembered Faye telling her this afternoon to take heed of her own advice. Did Catherine want to spend an entire lifetime pining for the man she loved?

The cab rolled forward just as she was hit with an acute understanding that could only be described as miraculous.

"Driver, stop!"

She pushed open the door, got out and turned to see Andy standing on the sidewalk looking at her quizzically.

"Could you store my bags?" she called out to him. "There's someone I need to see."

Andy's mouth split with a lopsided grin as he hurried back to the car. "Sounds like you're getting ready to do something crazy."

She smiled back. "You're absolutely right."

The state of Portland General's ER could have been described as a well-organized madhouse any day or night of the week. Weekends and holidays could be a bit worse, but every shift found doctors and nurses rushing to give patients in need some of the best emergency treatment that could be found in the Pacific Northwest. Tonight, however, the buzz in the ER wing seemed to have been kicked up a notch, all because an ambulance had arrived with an unconscious patient whose life had been saved with a steak knife and an ink pen. When the pneumatic doors opened and the surgeon himself waltzed in, the commotion elevated to a whole new level.

The attending physician had been so impressed with Riley's skillful handiwork that he'd called the ER Chief of Staff at home and told him he needed to come to the hospital and check it out.

It seemed that everyone on duty wanted to stop in to chat with Riley about his experience and to take a look at the patient. Riley was actually relieved for the chance to talk shop in the ER, and he let himself become consumed. That was much better than dwelling on the dark thoughts hovering at the edges of his brain.

When he caught sight of Dr. Richard Strong exiting one of the exam rooms at the far end of the hall, Riley was mildly surprised. He excused himself from the group of doctors and nurses.

"Richard," he called.

There was tension etched in the man's face.

Riley asked, "Is everything all right?"

"It's Jason," Richard said, looking relieved for someone to talk to. "My son. He was involved in a car accident. The doctor says he thinks Jason will be fine. But head injuries are so unpredictable that it's scary, you know?"

Riley nodded.

"They've taken him down for a CAT scan," Richard continued.

"Is he conscious?"

"Yes." Richard meandered toward the bank of elevators and the large window just a few yards away. Riley followed. "Conscious and able to communicate. I've been told that's an excellent sign."

"That's the truth." Then Riley remembered his discussion with Richard this afternoon. "You said you were meeting Jason for the first time tonight."

Strong shoved his hands into his pockets. "Yeah. Can you believe we met in the ER?" His smile was shaky with the aftermath of emotion. "That boy is something else, let me tell you. I was scared half to death. I rushed into that exam room to see this huge bandage on his head and glass fragments in his hair, and what does my son do? He cracks a joke. He looks me right in the eye and says, 'You'll have to excuse my appearance. I had a small mishap.' A small mishap." Richard shook his head, grinning. "Then he turns to his mother and starts swearing up and down that he wasn't to blame for the accident. He was trying to calm our fears, I guess. Trying to make us see that he was okay and that we should stop worrying."

Riley said, "Thoughtful kid."

"Carrie started crying and I laughed. Then Carrie

laughed and I got all choked up. We were wrecks." Richard sighed, twisting to stretch his neck to the left, then to the right. "You know, you find out you have a kid, and your whole world changes. But you find out your kid's in trouble, and everything that you thought was important means absolutely nothing."

The man was beginning to ramble. Riley knew the signs; the far-off glaze in the eyes, the gradual relaxing of the body, the voicing of profound thoughts, the re-evaluation of priorities. Riley had witnessed it a thousand times during his residency. After discovering that their loved ones would be okay, people slowly decelerated from a state of high anxiety.

"I don't have any children of my own," Riley told him, "but I can imagine how that would be true."

The doors of the elevator parted just as the bell announced its arrival. An orderly pushed a huge gurney out into the hallway right in front of them.

"There he is now." Richard's voice brightened considerably at the sight of his son. Riley didn't have to be told this was Jason. He looked a lot like Richard.

A white bandage slashed across the young man's forehead and temple. A small line of blood showed through.

"Yup," Jason said, grinning easily. "Seems I'm going to live."

Apparently, the sound of the elevator bell had Carrie checking the hallway. The instant she saw her son, she came rushing toward them. "So my boy's going to be all right?"

"I promised you I would be, didn't I?" Jason's teasing caused the anxiety on Carrie's face to ease.

"You did." She latched on to her son's hand, following the gurney back toward the exam room. "Hello, Dr. Jacobs," she said. "Have you met Jason? He's my pride and joy."

"I haven't." Riley looked at the young man. "How are you?"

"Believe me," Jason quipped, reaching up to touch the area of his wound tenderly, "I feel much better than I look."

The kid had a good attitude, Riley had to give him that. And he was devoted to his mother. It showed in the way his eyes lit up when he looked at her. But he seemed a tad uncertain about Richard. Jason kept casting quick, nervous glances at the man. Riley guessed that was quite natural since father and son were just getting to know each other.

Richard had moved around next to Carrie, and Riley couldn't help but notice how the three of them made a nice-looking little family. When they reached the door, Riley bid them all goodbye.

Then he remembered the NoWait he'd picked up off the table at the pub, and he was struck with the overpowering urge just to be rid of it.

"Richard," he said from the exam room doorway, "can I talk to you?"

Falling into step beside Riley in the empty hallway, Richard said, "What can I do for you?"

Riley stopped, reached into his pocket and pulled out the blue vial. "I was wondering if you could take this back to the lab when you go."

"Where'd you get this?" Richard asked.

Riley's jaw tensed. "Let's just say someone I know wanted to give NoWait a try. I confiscated it but not before we experienced some impressive results." He frowned. "I'll be very interested to see the data you come up with in the testing. That stuff is pretty powerful."

"Powerful?" Richard shook his head. "Nah. This stuff isn't going to do anything."

"What?" Riley was confused. "What do you mean? It's NoWait. It came from the lab."

"Oh, it came from the lab all right. But the oil in the blue vials is the placebo. The control. It's nothing more than vitamin E. Faye told me about it today. The techs haven't prepared the vials of NoWait yet."

"No way," Riley argued.

It couldn't be true. Riley remembered his romantic evening with Catherine, and how things had so quickly turned mind-numbingly explosive when they'd kissed and touched and—

"That's NoWait, Richard. It's got to be."

Richard uncapped the vial and took a whiff. He shook his head. "No. There's no scent. See for yourself."

He held it out, and Riley leaned forward and sniffed. No odor whatsoever. He knew full well that a fragrance had been added to NoWait. A pleasant, citrusy smell with a hint of musk.

"That's a problem we're going to have to deal with," Richard explained. "Making the control smell like the original NoWait so that the volunteers won't know whether they have the real thing or the placebo."

The implications of what Riley was learning were slow to sink in. He stood there staring at the vial.

"Whatever experience you—" Richard stopped and quickly corrected himself. "Whoever it was you took this from had an experience that had nothing to do with No-Wait."

"But…" Riley let the thought peter out. He couldn't even remember what he'd been about to say.

"Hey, buddy—" Richard gently punched him on the

shoulder "—a person can't complain about good sex. Right?"

Dumbfounded, Riley just nodded. He offered a vague goodbye and then headed down the hall that led to the lobby.

"Excuse me," a woman said. "Are you Dr. Riley Jacobs?"

Riley was still too stupefied to do anything but nod.

"I'm Suzanne Smith from the *Oregonian*. I hear you're some kind of doctor." She grinned. "From what I'm told, you've got astounding dexterity with ordinary eating utensils. Would you answer a few questions?"

Riley was still standing with the note-taking journalist when the ER Chief called out to him from the doorway that separated the inner workings of the ER from the lobby and waiting area.

"Excuse me," Riley said to the reporter, relieved to have an escape. "I have to go."

Apparently, the woman knew Riley was being summoned by the department head. "Dr. Hall's the boss around here, isn't he? Think he'd answer a few questions for the article?" As a carrot, she added, "It'll make for some good press for Portland General."

"I can't promise," Riley told her, "but I'll certainly ask."

"Thanks," the reporter called after him.

Dr. Thomas Hall was the man under whom Riley had worked during his residency here at the ER. Hall was a perfectionist who expected only the best. Working for him had been difficult, but Riley owed a lot to the man's tough standards.

They shook hands.

"She from the *Oregonian?*" Dr. Hall asked, indicating the reporter several yards behind Riley.

"I think so." He couldn't admit that he'd been in such a fog that he couldn't remember the name of the paper or the journalist. "She'd like to talk to you." Riley felt suddenly uncomfortable being the center of attention. It was one thing to discuss his ordeal with colleagues, but talking to the media was different. "She thinks this is newsworthy."

"It is." Dr. Hall looked over Riley's shoulder, waving to the reporter and letting her know he'd be with her shortly. Then he turned his attention back to Riley.

"I've already looked in on your patient." Dr. Hall draped a congratulatory arm around Riley's shoulder and drew him to a private corner that afforded some privacy. "That is one amazing story. Is it true you used an ink pen to release the pressure in his chest cavity?"

"Spur-of-the-moment thinking." Riley shrugged as he offered the excuse.

Dr. Hall laughed. "Good work. I guess you know the guy's doing well."

"Yes, and I'm happy to hear it."

"Listen, Riley," Dr. Hall said as he took a step backward, his tone lowering, "I've been kicking myself ever since I let Graham steal you away from me and plant you over there in the clinic. You belong here."

Riley went still. He'd like nothing better than to return to practicing emergency medicine. But he didn't want to get his hopes up.

"Your talent is being wasted over there at the Healthy Living Clinic."

There had been a time not too long ago when Riley would have agreed. But in that instant, Riley thought of Catherine, remembered how she'd made him understand that, even though he wasn't treating trauma patients or dealing with emergencies that required swift and competent solutions, he *had* helped the people over at the clinic who had come seeking better, healthier lifestyles.

Riley felt the need to say, "There's some good work going on over there, Dr. Hall."

"I'm sure there is. And from what I hear, you've done a great job of getting things back on track." He crossed his arms over his chest. "But with all that said, would you be willing to come work for me? You'd be an asset to the ER team. I'll get you over here really quick. All you have to do is say the word. Would you be willing?"

"Willing? Are you kidding? Working over here is what I wanted all along." A job in Portland General's ER would fulfill a dream for him. "But I'm afraid Graham might balk at your moving his chess pieces before he's ready."

"Doesn't matter," Dr. Hall said. "That pedestal he's created for himself is getting shaky, if you know what I mean. He's abused his position for a long time now. His reign is nearly over."

Riley didn't think it proper to ask any further questions. But he had no reason to doubt Dr. Hall's word. The man was well-respected—much more so than David Graham—and he was known to be part of the inner circle of those who ran the hospital. Besides that, he'd been practicing at the hospital for over twenty-five years and had an impeccable reputation.

Dr. Hall's tone lowered. "I want you to know that the administrators are aware of how Dr. Graham misled you. We know why he put you over there."

"What do you mean?"

Dr. Hall looked mildly surprised. "He was looking for a scapegoat should scandal hit the clinic. But we wouldn't have let you take the fall, Riley," Dr. Hall told him. "We've been watching, monitoring. We also know about how Graham's been treating Dr. Lassen. How he's withheld what she's been due for a long time."

Riley frowned, feeling as though he was in some kind of war zone and being hit from all sides. It was nothing but pure irritability that had him asking, "So why is Dr. Graham's behavior being tolerated? I don't understand."

"It isn't easy to oust the hospital's director." A tiny smile quirked Dr. Hall's mouth. "We're giving him rope."

And allowing the man to hang himself. The unspoken words were clear.

Riley nodded in understanding.

"I heard that Graham persuaded you to go over to the clinic by holding your past over your head."

Riley refused to break eye contact with the man. Riley was confident in his medical proficiency. He deserved to be respected for that alone. Still, he couldn't deny the self-consciousness stalking him.

"As black marks go, Riley," Dr. Hall continued, "the one you've got in your past is quite small. I don't want you thinking it's going to keep you from getting ahead here. You're going to have a successful career. Because you deserve it. You're a talented doctor. That's all that matters."

Riley felt as if a great weight had been lifted off his shoulders.

"Dr. Jacobs."

Riley turned to face the nurse who had hailed him.

"There's someone asking for you," she said. "I told her she couldn't come back here. That she'd have to wait in the lobby."

"It's probably that reporter," Dr. Hall said. "She's thought of more questions for you. Tell her I'll be right out, too. I have to make a quick call first."

As Riley headed down the hall, he realized he didn't feel up to answering any more questions. He should be feeling good. He'd soon be working in his dream job. He'd be part of the ER team. But his steps were heavy and he felt as if he was enveloped in a cloud, gray and bleak.

He glanced at his watch. It was late. Surely Catherine was at the airport by now. Soon she'd be boarding a plane that would fly her back to Lextanya.

It was for the best, he realized, turning the corner and pushing open the door that would take him to the waiting room. He only regretted that Catherine would never know that the flames that had blazed between them last night hadn't been fueled by anything except the desire they felt for each other.

Riley lifted his gaze, expecting to see the reporter. But he didn't. It was Catherine who stood there waiting. And although he knew her being here was probably the worst thing for her, he couldn't deny the pure pleasure that permeated his being, soul-deep.

Fourteen

Catherine's insides felt all quivery. Seeing Riley made her feel both wonderful and dreadful. Wonderful, because she'd come to some very significant realizations about him, about her life. Dreadful, because she knew there was nothing she could say that would earn his forgiveness for what she'd done.

"Shouldn't you be at the airport?" he asked.

There was no anger in his voice, and she was grateful for that. But she had the sudden worry that he'd grown apathetic. Could he have become indifferent to her so quickly?

The question only amplified her apprehension.

"I'm not going home." She moistened her dry lips and hoped she could keep her anguished tears at bay until she was able to explain. If he even let her explain.

Catherine wrung her hands. "Can we talk?"

"Come on." His hand on her arm was gentle as he led her toward the pneumatic doors of the lobby. "Let's take a walk. I've been cooped up in the hospital for hours."

The cool breeze blew from the west.

"You chilly?" he asked.

"I'll be all right."

He slid his jacket off and draped it over her shoulders. The warm scent of him clung to the fabric, and Catherine breathed it in.

"I couldn't go, Riley. I couldn't leave with things so messed up. I needed to talk to you. I needed to apologize."

He groaned, stopping right there on the sidewalk and turning her to face him. "Let's not do this."

"But I have to," she insisted. "I don't want you thinking I'm that kind of person. Someone who does anything to get what she wants. I'm no manipulator, Riley. I don't lie, I don't cheat and I don't behave recklessly." Upon thinking about it, she decided to add, "Normally I don't, anyway."

His mouth twitched, and she realized he was curbing a smile. Was he so impassive toward her that he could actually laugh at her distress? Fear welled up in her, but she tamped it down. She'd come here to speak her mind and she intended to do just that.

"I want you to know that it's all your fault," she blurted.

The accusation wiped all trace of a smile off his handsome face.

"That's not what I meant," she hurried to say. "Or rather that's not *exactly* what I meant." She paused long enough to swallow, and then she tried again. "It's because of you— It's because I *met* you that—" Frustration set in. "You made me do things—"

This wasn't coming out right at all.

Just say the words, a firm voice in her head commanded.

"Riley, I think I love you." She squared her shoulders. "No. There's no thinking about it. I know I love you."

He closed his eyes and exhaled, his shoulders rounding.

Trepidation lumped in her throat. He was taking this as if it were terrible news. And why shouldn't he, after what she'd done?

"Come on." He sounded hoarse as he took her hand and started off down the street again.

They walked a full block in silence. She could feel a gloominess fairly pulsating off him. Finally, she couldn't stand it any longer. He'd been quiet for too, too long.

"Riley, I understand your being unable to forgive me. But I never would have done something like that unless—"

"It's not that."

"You're not upset about last night? You forgive me?"

She forced him to stop. She needed him to look at her. His eyes would tell her the truth.

His dark gaze was steady and sincere. She detected not a wisp of anger in him. Catherine sighed with relief, her breath leaving her in a grateful rush. She pressed the flat of her hand to the base of her throat. "I can't tell you how relieved I am. But if you're not angry with me, what's wrong? You look so unhappy."

She suspected it was habit alone that had him glancing down the empty street before stepping off the curb to cross.

"I am unhappy," he admitted. "It's because I…"

The rest of his sentence faded. Frantic to know what he was thinking, she urged, "Because you what?"

"Here." His grasp on her hand unwittingly firmed as they stepped up onto the sidewalk. "Let's sit down for a minute."

The bench was illuminated by the soft yellow glow of a streetlamp. The spot was a stop on the city bus route, but the buses had finished running for the night.

"Catherine," Riley slowly began, "I have never met a woman quite like you. You've made an incredible impact on my life. And in such a short time."

He paused, and she got the impression that he, too, felt frustrated.

"There's more I want to say—" his mouth flattened for a second and he shook his head "—but I don't think I should."

"Of course, you should," she softly but urgently insisted.

After a moment of hesitation, he continued, "I'm surprised by how much I— You've come to mean a lot— I really think that I—"

Catherine felt breathless. "Riley, are you trying to tell me that you feel the same way I do? That you love me, too?"

He nodded, but he looked too damned sad.

She settled farther back on the bench with a heavy sigh. "Realizing we're in love should be a wonderful thing, yet both of us are depressed. I can understand you feeling that way after what I've done. And besides that, no one in his right mind would want to get mixed up with me and my crazy family, or my chaotic way of life with all its outrageous rules and regulations."

"It's not that," he said. "It's not that at all."

"Then what?" She was confused.

He leaned away from her a fraction. "Let's just say that I wouldn't be welcomed by your family."

"Your not being an aristocrat will be hard for my father to swallow, I'll admit." Her thoughts started churning. "I could call my cousin. Max would help me to convince Father—" A sudden idea rose in her head, bright as dawn. "Max's wife isn't a noble. He met her right here in Portland. I don't know why I didn't think of this before. The King, himself, set a new standard by marrying the woman he loved. I certainly should be able to do the same, don't you think?"

But the expression on Riley's face took the wind out of her sails.

"It's not because I'm a regular Joe, Catherine."

"That's why I love you. Because you are a regular Joe." She smiled and tried to draw closer to him, but he held her from him.

"You don't understand."

"Then make me understand, Riley."

He fell silent for so long that she began to worry. But she forced herself to wait until he was ready.

"I have a record, Catherine. A criminal record."

She sat still, uncertain about how to respond.

"I was young," he continued, "and stupid. Seventeen and desperate to find a way to get some kind of response out of my father. It took years of court-ordered counseling for me to unearth that little gold nugget. Dad was a workaholic with two jobs. He spent so many hours away from home during the years I was growing up that I don't have a single memory of us doing anything together. Of course, I had my mother. But she'd been raised with three sisters and she didn't have any idea what to do with a boisterous boy.

"By the time I hit my teens, I was angry and rebellious. I got in with the wrong crowd and started stealing. Not that I needed the things I took. At the time, I thought I was looking for a thrill. But later my counselor made me understand that the fact that I was so blatantly obvious about breaking the law only meant that I wanted to get caught. And I believe that to be the truth. I wanted to force my father to come to the police station. And that's just what happened."

Riley sighed. "Petty theft is what I was convicted of. I didn't do any actual time. The judge insisted I be tried as an adult. He sentenced me with a hefty fine and three hundred hours of community service, plus counseling."

Catherine could keep silent no longer. "How did your father react?"

Shrugging, Riley said, "He didn't say much of anything. He just paid the fine and went back to work."

"Oh, Riley. I'm sorry." It seemed that parents could damage their children so easily. And they probably didn't even realize what they were doing.

"My father and I were able to reach an understanding," Riley said softly. "Just a few months after my court appearance, Dad came home early from work. I was there but Mom was out." Almost to himself, he added, "For the life of me, I can't remember where she'd gone. Anyway, Dad told me he wasn't feeling well. He was pale, sweaty and seemed to have trouble breathing. Then he got worse. When he complained of chest pains, I helped him to the car and drove him to Portland General."

The moment turned tense. Catherine watched as Riley smoothed his palms up and down his thighs.

"The doctors revived Dad," he continued. "But something happened. There was something about Dad. It was like…he knew. He knew his time had come. I was sick to my stomach seeing him lying there so helpless. As angry as I'd been at him, I'd have done anything to keep him from dying.

"He caught my eye and in that one, silent moment, he

expressed years and years of unspoken sentiment. He loved me. I could see it as plain as day. And he regretted bitterly all the years we'd missed together."

He shook his head, leaning forward to rest his elbows on his knees. "Now, the message that was received could have all been due to the hopeful dreams of a desperate teenager, but I choose to think differently. My father realized he'd made a mistake, and he wanted me to know it, too."

"Your father died?"

He nodded, reclining against the back of the bench. "He had a second heart attack and it took his life. But not before he whispered a message. 'Make me proud, Riley,' he said."

Moist emotion glittered in Riley's gaze. Catherine reached out and slipped her hand under his biceps, scooting over to hug his arm tightly.

"Those four little words changed my life, Catherine. Dad's request turned me around. And I was so amazed by the doctors in the ER who worked on my father." His head shook in wonder. "They inspired me. I wanted to become a doctor. I wanted to help people, to give them more time to live." His voice became raspy as he added, "More time to love."

Tears rolled down Catherine's face.

The soles of Riley's shoes scuffed against the sidewalk. "After Dad died, I started studying hard. It was difficult because I'd been such a slacker up to that point. But I had the help of a dedicated counselor, and several of my teachers became mentors, too. I was accepted into college. My criminal record nearly kept me out of med school, but I went to see the judge who had sentenced me, and asked him for a letter of recommendation. That was what clinched it for me, I think."

Catherine couldn't help but murmur, "You're sure it wasn't the sheer determination on your part?"

Riley smiled. "Could have been. I was determined to become a doctor. To practice emergency medicine." His voice was raw as he added, "To make my dad proud."

"It's an honorable motivation, Riley. I'm sorry I gave you such a hard time about your attitude on working in the clinic."

"Don't apologize," he told her. "How were you to know that I'd been forced into taking the job?"

"You might not have wanted to be there, but the clinic is thriving," she commented.

"I can only take minimal credit for what's happening in the clinic. Faye is the top dog over there. Or she should be, anyway."

"She does work hard."

Riley smiled, and Catherine was relieved that the conversation had moved on to a less distressing topic.

"I'm pretty sure she's going to get a promotion."

"Oh?"

"I'm leaving the clinic. I've been offered a position in the ER."

She gave his arm a squeeze. "Congratulations, Riley. I'm so happy for you."

"It's strange. I should be happy, too."

She pulled back and looked up into his face. "You're not?"

"I wasn't unhappy when the offer was made," he said. "But something was missing."

His gaze was on her then, intense with concentrated emotion.

"I've figured out that the something was you."

Her only thought was to kiss him. But when she leaned in, he tenderly captured her jaw between his fingers.

"This won't work." Regret clouded his gaze. "You don't want to disappoint your father. You don't want your family's name splashed all over the tabloids by marrying beneath you."

"'Beneath me'? That sounds horrible. You don't honestly believe that, do you?"

His smile was sad. "I don't, no. But your father would never accept a son-in-law with a criminal record."

"I don't see how he can complain," she quipped, "since his own daughter has one, too." The utter surprise on his handsome face made her chuckle.

"I told you I was a lonely, wretched teenager," she explained. "I was overweight and had few friends. Well, I was approached by a group of popular girls who promised to make me a member of their club. However, I had to fulfill a dare. I was caught red-handed. Literally. The policeman walked right up to me while I was spray painting the club insignia. I had the paint can in hand, wet red paint running to my elbow." She screwed up her nose. "The nozzle got stuck.

"Father was livid," she continued. "I've never seen him so angry. An article had just run in the newspaper suggesting corruption in our judiciary system. Father felt he had no recourse but to hold a special counsel, which he presided over. The place was packed, reporters everywhere. I was only sixteen. And talk about mortified."

She shook her head. She could laugh about it now, but at the time it had been a nightmare.

"Father sentenced me to five hundred hours of volunteer service."

Riley whistled. "Stiff sentence for a little graffiti."

"I defaced a national memorial."

"Catherine!"

"I know. I was terrible."

He laughed, and her brows arched high.

"I'm sorry." But he didn't sound it. "It's funny. You have to admit it. A princess with a criminal record."

Her mouth split into a grin, and then she, too, chuckled. "I know. It is funny. Now. But I did learn a huge lesson…"

In unison, they said, "Don't get caught." Their laughter rang into the night.

"Seriously, though," she told him, "it might have been a difficult time, but my volunteer service exposed me to the needs of the children in Lextanya. Since then I've been building community centers all over my country. It's very rewarding work."

Sometime during their conversation, they'd cuddled close, their fingers were laced, and it seemed the most natural thing in the world for Catherine to rest her head on his shoulder.

She wanted this man. Loved him with every fiber of her being.

Niggling doubt had her changing the subject and she asked, "Do you think we'd have made love without the No-Wait?"

Riley twisted to face her, clasping his hands on her upper arms. "I completely forgot to tell you. The oil in that vial wasn't NoWait. It was nothing more than vitamin E. That's the placebo they're using for the testing."

Her eyes widened. "You mean that was…"

"Just us," he provided.

A wicked grin curled her lips. "Wow," she said, her tone throaty with sudden sensuality, "I can't wait to try that again."

Desire lit his dark eyes. "That's what I'm thinking."

"Let's fly to Rio, Riley," she said. "Or let's drive to Vegas. I don't want anything to keep us apart. I want—"

"Hold it," he snapped, and for a quick instant she thought he was angry. But then he calmly said, "Are you asking me to marry you?"

"Well, I've been sitting here forever waiting for you to pop the question." She shrugged.

He didn't laugh as she'd expected. Instead, he soberly asked, "But what about that guy over there who's waiting for you? And what about your father?"

"I'm not saying there aren't problems. But if we're together, there's no problem we can't overcome." She reached up and slipped her arms around his neck.

He kissed her then, his lips urgent and demanding.

Breathlessly she whispered, "Is that a yes?"

He smiled against her mouth. "That, my love, is a yes."

Epilogue

Catherine accepted the helping hand of a footman as she stepped down from the majestically decorated horse-drawn carriage. Faye Lassen, looking lovely in her narrow-cut bridesmaid dress, held Catherine's massive white rose bouquet while attendants scurried to straighten her gorgeous wedding gown and unfurl the yards of lacy fabric that made up her train. The crowd outside the cathedral cheered and, as was customary during a royal wedding, tossed fresh flowers in her path.

"I know I've already said this at least a dozen times today," Faye said, "but you look beautiful. Are you nervous?"

"Actually," Catherine whispered so as not to be overheard, "I'd just like to get this over with. I've been an old married woman for four months now."

Although they hadn't been the easiest four months, she

could honestly say she'd never been happier in her life. Needless to say, her father had been less than pleased to learn that she and Riley had eloped to Vegas where they'd pledged their vows in a cozy little wedding chapel. She'd heard that her father had commented that such a wedding could be nothing but tacky, but he couldn't have been more wrong.

Her father had eventually come around to the idea of having Riley as a son-in-law, however. He'd had no choice, really. Catherine was pleased with her own quick thinking; she had called Max and had him deliver the news personally. Prince Wilhelm couldn't very well rant at his sovereign, now, could he?

By the time Catherine and Riley had flown to Lextanya for a visit a few days later, her father had calmed down enough to speak civilly. The Prince had insisted on a formal wedding. When Catherine had suggested she share the day with Yvonne in a double ceremony, her father had actually seemed pleased with his older daughter.

Not even a double wedding could surpass Max's coronation, but the Prince intended to make the day a lavish celebration. The event would be archived as Lextanya's only double royal wedding to date. Or would that be the only royal double wedding?

"Besides," Catherine complained to her friend, "I miss Riley."

Faye and Catherine had flown to Lextanya early for the traditional bridal trousseau shopping expedition. And although Catherine had talked to Riley every day, she hadn't seen him since she'd left Portland a whole week ago. She wanted her man—in every sense of the word!

Just the thought of the steamy nights she and Riley had spent in each other's arms made her ache with need.

The carriage that had transported her from the castle pulled away from the cobblestone curve. Catherine glanced down the street to see Yvonne's carriage approaching. Prince Wilhelm wouldn't have been happy unless his daughters rode in separate royal coaches.

"Well, Riley's in the church waiting for you," Faye told her.

Catherine smiled. "There's someone in there waiting for you, too."

Joy brightened Faye's face. "Mark? You flew Mark over?"

Faye and her husband were slowly working out their problems. And Catherine was happy to have had a hand in getting them back together.

Changes had started taking place back in Portland almost immediately after Riley and Catherine had returned from Las Vegas. David Graham had been forced into retirement, Riley was once again working in the ER and Faye had taken over the running of the clinic.

The staff had organized a reception for Faye, and Catherine had done a bit of research to find Mark Lassen. Catherine had slipped an invitation in the mail for Mark, and he'd shown up at the party. Faye and Mark had been together ever since.

The NoWait testing was still going on, and probably would be for years yet. Carrie Martin had moved to Portland to be with Richard Strong, and in addition to working at the clinic, Dr. Richie had launched a self-help talk show on a local cable channel. He hawked videos of himself on a wide variety of topics from weight control to addictions to sexual dysfunction. However, the man had changed drastically. He was less focused on fame and fortune and more concerned with helping people.

Catherine continued to attend seminars at the clinic and work out at the gym there. The community of Portland General Hospital and the Healthy Living Clinic seemed to have settled back to normal. But she continued to hear fantastic stories about the aphrodisiac side-effects of Dr. Richie's miracle oil. Several couples had met and married because of NoWait, and everyone was waiting to see just how many babies might be born because of the stuff.

Faye handed Catherine her bouquet just as the second carriage pulled to a stop in front of the ancient cathedral. Yvonne stepped out, a grand vision in her pristine white gown. The sisters hugged and then proceeded up the steps to where their father waited to lead them down the aisle.

When the women reached him, Prince Wilhelm blessed both his daughters with a bright smile. The three of them entered the church.

The pews were packed with family, friends and important dignitaries, and hauntingly beautiful music from the pipe organ filled the lofty space. Catherine wanted to race up the aisle, but forced herself to behave with the decorum that would make her family proud.

Then she saw him. The man she loved. The man of her dreams. The man of her heart.

He looked good in his royal garb. The scarlet waistcoat was complete with shiny gold buttons and fancy epaulets especially made for Lextanyan royalty. After today Riley Jacobs wouldn't be a regular Joe any longer.

Thankfully, the people of Lextanya had welcomed and accepted Riley from the first moment he'd stepped off the plane. This was a country of romantics, thank goodness. Keeping their elopement a secret from the tabloids had been impossible, but that hadn't seemed to matter. Apparently, all of this was a beloved fairy tale to her people, an enchanted love story that they simply could not get enough of.

Having the chance to remarry the love of her life was like being handed a luscious dessert after she'd already binged on a scrumptious meal.

Dipping her chin, she zeroed in on Riley and did her best to communicate to him silently her every desperate longing. It felt as if she hadn't seen him for a solid month rather than a mere seven days.

Love glittered in his brown eyes, and she could tell that he, too, had been missing her. Elation filled her heart, setting it pattering, as each step took her closer to her happily ever after.

* * * * *

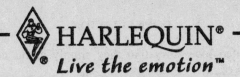

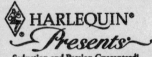
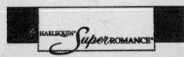

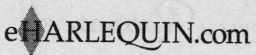

Harlequin Historicals®
Historical Romantic Adventure!

From rugged lawmen and valiant knights to defiant heiresses and spirited frontierswomen, Harlequin Historicals will capture your imagination with their dramatic scope, passion and adventure.

Harlequin Historicals . . . they're too good to miss!

HARLEQUIN®
INTRIGUE®

WE'LL LEAVE YOU BREATHLESS!

If you've been looking for thrilling tales of
contemporary passion and sensuous love stories
with taut, edge-of-the-seat suspense—then
you'll love Harlequin Intrigue!

Every month, you'll meet six new heroes
who are guaranteed to make your spine tingle
and your pulse pound. With them you'll enter
into the exciting world of Harlequin Intrigue—
where your life is on the line
and so is your heart!

THAT'S INTRIGUE—
ROMANTIC SUSPENSE
AT ITS BEST!

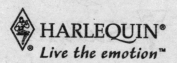

HARLEQUIN®
Live the emotion™

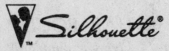